A Sleigh Ride Kiss

JEN GEIGLE JOHNSON

KINGS ROW PRESS

FOLLOW JEN

Jen's other published books

The Duke's Second Chance
The Earl's Winning Wager
Her Lady's Whims and Whimsies
Suitors for the Proper Miss
Pining for Lord Lockhart
The Foibles and Follies of Miss Grace

The Nobleman's Daughter
Two lovers in disguise

Scarlet
The Pimpernel retold

A Lady's Maid
Can she love again?

His Lady in Hiding
Hiding out as his maid.

Spun of Gold
Rumpelstilskin Retold

Dating the Duke
Time Travel: Regency man in NYC

Charmed by His Lordship
The antics of a fake friendship

Tabitha's Folly
Four over-protective brothers

To read Damen's Secret
The Villain's Romance

Follow her Newsletter

A CHRISTMAS MATCH

A Wish for Father Christmas
A Sleigh Ride Kiss
A Yuletide Carol
A Misteltoe Mismatch
A Tangled Wreath

CHAPTER 1

DECEMBER 1, 1815

*M*iss Odette Goodson told herself that everything she could possibly need was right there in Cheshire County. The rocky hills, rolling green, and tall pines were quite sufficient. With a dear grandmother who loved her and a comfortable home, what more could she want or expect from life? Most certainly, she was perfectly satisfied. She repeated her mantra over in her mind. Happy indeed.

After traipsing through the back part of her neighbor, the Marquis', estate, she crossed the bridge that entered her property line. Her customary pause led her to snatch up a stick and toss it in the water, surely it could go out on grand adventures. She watched it travel down the creek and out of sight. She'd found almost all corners and unused copses of trees on that estate and was running out of new areas to discover within walking distance. The family wouldn't mind, though. No one was there to even care at the moment. The Missing Marquis was still missing as far as she could tell. His dear mother had passed away this past year; everyone for miles in any direction had attended her funeral. Everyone except her son. Odette had met the mother, but didn't really know any of the family particularly well. She'd

1

been gone herself for much of her time growing up in Cheshire. But her grandmother Amelie counted them as dear friends.

Her long walk had kept her warm in the chilly air, so warm her cheeks flushed. Her hands were well protected in the mittens Grandmother had knitted. And she'd never worn so many stockings under countless skirts. She wondered if any woman felt the chill with all the clothing involved in preparing for the weather.

How many times had her grandmother reminded her to wear a pelisse, or bring an umbrella, or be certain she didn't ruin her slippers? It seemed the woman's one task was to see to Odette's presentation every time she crossed the threshold to brave the outdoors.

Odette smiled. But she loved that woman. She'd never met a single soul quite like her grandmother.

Odette breathed deeply the fresh, earthy air. Pine trees, the lovely kings of their property, towered in evergreen majesty all around her. Their yellow and green pine cones lay at her feet, tumbling about ahead of her when her toe connected with one, and the air was crisp with their nutty smell. She attempted to commit the beauty around her to memory so she could recount it to her dear guardian. Grandmother didn't enjoy long walks anymore.

The quiet was just what she had needed. With just the two of them living in the home and a generally quiet atmosphere, Grandmother had been talking lately about the virtues of marriage. Odette had graduated from finishing school and was now home to stay, just in time for the holidays and, she had recently learned, to prepare for her first Season.

Odette didn't feel ready for a Season. Grandmother had said they could *start* with the families who lived close. But her heart was set on a London Season for her granddaughter. "Marry well and you will live your days in peaceful bliss."

She knew Grandmother was correct, of course.

Odette's boots crackled on the frozen ground as she walked

down the lane that cut across their property. Bells jingled just around the bend. Sleigh bells. But there wasn't enough snow for a sleigh. She stepped off the lane to watch and see who might be coming.

A smaller equipage with two horses bounced along on the lane in such a cheery approach that she laughed. Until she noticed the man holding the reins. It was one thing to be caught smiling on the side of the path for no apparent reason when the witness was a friendly neighbor or an older matron, but to find a man...Her cheeks flushed further, and not from the cold. She was certain she looked positively with fever. He was young and handsome and nothing like she'd ever seen before. And she was standing alone on the side of the road, smiling like a simpleton. But there was nothing for it, and nowhere to hide, so she stood up taller and lifted her chin.

He made a low, soothing sound, and the horses stopped. Their air came out in puffs of white. His scarf was red, his hat black, and his jacket a dark hunter green. He looked like Father Christmas himself, and Odette was filled with an irrational desire to laugh again.

He dipped his head. "Good afternoon."

"And to you." She dipped in a quick curtsey, unsure how she should be greeting this stranger.

"Might I offer you a ride?"

"Oh." She looked all around them. Was that a proper enough thing to do? They were well and truly alone. But no one would mind or have a care. She could be dropped a bit closer to the house, but perhaps not right in front. Grandmother need not see this reckless moment with a stranger. "Thank you. Yes, please."

"Excellent." He leapt down and offered his hand. The steps were high and steep, but he eased the way so expertly that she was soon sitting on the bench without trouble. He joined her, and then she realized her folly. For he sat very close indeed. And they were very much alone.

3

But his smile was jolly. "I can take you home directly, or we can enjoy this beautiful, crisp air for a moment first." His eyes twinkled like no one's she had ever seen. Surely, a man such as he could bring no harm.

"I'm Miss Odette Goodson."

"Pleased to meet you, Miss Goodson. You may call me Henry Wardlow if you like."

"Thank you." She didn't know anyone by that name. Although, she hardly knew anyone. Their neighbor, the elder Marquis of Wilmington, had been a dear friend to her grandmother before he passed, and except for a few others, Odette knew precious few in the neighborhood. Wardlow. Who were the Wardlows? "Are you new?"

"I am, in a way. I've just arrived, at any rate. The air was so beautiful, and these fine animals were clamoring for some exercise. I cannot ride them both at once."

"No, that is true. And tell me, Mr. Henry Wardlow, are you a safe sort of person?"

He burst into great laughter at her question, which brought out a bit of her own. "I did not wish to be quite so amusing."

"No, of course not. But I can assure you that I am indeed a mostly safe sort of person."

Mostly safe? Something about the way he said it, and the look of teasing in his eyes, made her wonder if she would in fact enjoy his idea of mostly safe. "Well then, shall we go for a ride before dropping me off at home?"

"Most excellent." He dipped his hat. "I knew when I saw you that you would be the exploring type."

"Am I?"

"Most certainly. For aren't you far from home doing just such a thing right now?"

"I am, yes."

"And which of these estates is yours?"

"Not mine precisely, but we are currently on the Goodson estate, where I live with my grandmother."

"A fine family."

"Do you know the Goodsons?" How could he know her family when she'd heard nothing about him?

"I do indeed." He clucked and the horses moved forward. They clopped along again in the same dancing manner as before.

"You know, I think your horses enjoy this more than we do."

"I do believe you are correct. Although, I am enjoying things much more with such a jolly companion at my side."

She smiled. "Then I shall as well."

"Those two magnificent animals are attached. That's Ginger on the left and Bread on the right."

"You cannot be serious."

"Oh I am, and believe me, the horses' names are not ones to trifle with at my house."

"Certainly, I meant no offense."

"None taken." He turned them down a lane away from her estate. She smiled again.

"Tell me more about the area," Mr. Wardlow said. "I assume you've lived here all of your life?"

"Well, no. When I was but ten years of age, my parents passed away and I was sent to live with a most beloved grandmother. But she soon sent me away to finishing school. I might be of little use to you. What would you like to know about us?"

"Do the families dine? Are there any mysteries? Who is the town gossip?" His eyebrows wiggled around almost ridiculously on his face, but she could only laugh.

"The gossip, I don't know. I'm dreadfully uninformed."

"Then you are not her. You are not the town gossip."

She gasped. "Most certainly not."

He nodded. "Just so. But that tells me I won't get any information out of you."

She sighed. "You are likely correct. I would know more

5

about the trees and the gardens. Which have all grown in monumental amounts since I was last here." She peered at him to see his reaction, but he didn't seem bored in the slightest. Nor did he appear to think her odd.

"Then you must tell me all about the trees and the gardens."

She could hardly believe he was serious, so she began with the pines, half expecting the bored, glazed eyes of most anyone else she might have tried to discuss trees with. "These large, towering evergreens originated in Scotland."

"Did they? They're fabulous."

"They really are. They've certainly been here longer than we have." They turned off the lane and onto a wider, more used road, toward the tenants.

She wondered about her new acquaintance. They neared the first family, resettled from Wales. The Hugheses were silk weavers and tenants on the Goodson land.

To her great surprise, as soon as Mr. Wardlow pulled closer, Mrs. Hughes threw open the door with her hands clasped and her smile as large as Odette had ever seen it. "You're returned. Oh, my dear boy, I'm so happy to see you."

He pulled to a stop. "Would you mind terribly if we stop here?"

"Not at all. The Hugheses are a beloved family."

"They are." He was now completely focused on Mrs. Hughes. "How is one of my favorite families?"

She ran to him. "Come here, you dear boy. Though you're not a boy any longer, are you?"

Mr. Hughes came around the house. "I heard the missus getting herself excited, and now I see why. You've returned, lad. It's mighty good to see you."

"You, too, Mr. Hughes."

He embraced them both, and soon their chatter was fast and difficult to follow. But it sounded like Mr. Wardlow had been away for many years and was just now returning. Sounded like he had quite a lot to share and had a grand adventure. And it was also pretty obvious that he was, or used to be, a tenant of some sort.

Odette's disappointment was sharper than she expected. He was so well dressed, and driving a phaeton. She'd thought they might have been equals in station.

But now that she looked closer, his shoes were worn. His clothes were only festive, not necessarily the latest styles. And he could have borrowed the phaeton from someone of wealth.

Ah well. Grandmother had Odette's mind all awhirl with courtship. Every man she met need not be seen as a candidate.

When the Hugheses at last had a moment to spare, they smiled and greeted Odette as well. She almost laughed at the difference in their exuberance. She responded cheerfully enough. "Good to see you, Mrs. Hughes."

They were invited in profusely, over and over again, but Mr. Wardlow said that they needed to be going. "Thank you. I'll be returning. You know I will."

"Will you, though? It took ye all of eight years to come back this last time."

"Don't you worry, now. I'll not be taking those same journeys again." Did his voice take on a wistful tone?

They nodded and waved, watching until Mr. Wardlow had turned the corner.

"My goodness." Odette shook her head. "I have known the Hugheses my whole life, and never have I seen them quite so animated."

But Mr. Wardlow didn't explain. His small smile twitched in one corner, and he clucked at the horses.

They continued down the lane, Mr. Wardlow nodding at nearly every person who stepped outside their door.

They reached the main street in town, then he turned. "I think I need to make my way home. Shall we at last drop you home as well?"

"Yes, thank you. But I've enjoyed our outing very much."

"I'm pleased to hear that. I could never leave a lady standing by herself on the lane. What kind of gentleman would do such a thing?"

So, was he a gentleman? She studied him some more. He certainly had the manners of one. "Your parents have taught you well."

"Thank you. I feel I owe most of my deportment to my elderly great-aunt who stepped in when my parents grew tired of me. But thank you."

Perhaps he had a well-bred aunt?

No matter. Her grandmother would know about him. She knew everyone, knew their families, their roots, and where they were going. Was *she* the town gossip? Certainly not, not with the way she abhorred the practice. No, her grandmother knew everything about everyone because they told her themselves, or she made it her business to know.

And like Odette had thought almost every day, there was no one quite like her grandmother.

They pulled up right in front of her door.

Smithson opened the door as always, and a footman exited to help her down.

But Mr. Wardlow beat him to her side. "Please, allow me." He held up a hand.

"Oh, well, thank you very much."

Her grandmother's face in the window was amused at best, slightly horrified at worst. But Odette kept up a cheerful face for Mr. Wardlow. "I do appreciate the ride home, as well as the extra excursion."

"And I appreciated the company. Thank you." He bowed, and then climbed aboard his phaeton, clicked, and the horses were off again.

"What an interesting thing to happen." She watched him leave, and he didn't look back. Was he as intrigued as she? He didn't seem very interested. But then again, he would know their class difference.

If they had one.

Grandmother exited out onto the front drive. "Who was that?"

"Oh, Grandmother. I don't even know. He picked me up near the bridge. Seeing me alone, he assumed I would suffer to make the walk. And we drove by the row of tenants. You should have seen the Hugheses. They've never been more excited, I tell you." She shrugged. "I couldn't get too many details from him, but I assumed he was a former tenant somewhere here in Cheshire? Perhaps a part of the silk industry?"

"Oh no. If he's one of those mill owners, we can have nothing to do with him."

"Why would he be, with the Hugheses so excited . . ." The Hugheses were independent silk weavers. The mills were in competition for their customers. He didn't seem to fit anywhere in her mind.

"Who can know, really, which is precisely why you don't accept rides from strangers, and you certainly don't ride alone with men you don't know. Truly, a phaeton is a romantic option in a crowded park. Not down narrow lanes with no one else around." Grandmother huffed. "I know you certainly thought of these things when he helped you up inside."

"Not then, but once I was seated, I did, yes."

Grandmother nodded. "Well, at least you remembered."

"I did, certainly, and he was the happiest man, full of smiles and good humor. I just couldn't imagine him being the slightest risk."

"And those can be the worst danger, in more ways than you realize."

Odette agreed, only partly wondering what ways her grandmother might be referring to.

"But come in, let's have our supper early tonight, shall we?"

She tucked her hand on Odette's arm, her new way of moving about when Odette was present.

"Of course, are you well?" She stood close to her grandmother, ready to help steady her feet if need be.

"Perfectly well. I only wish to read my book."

Their evening sounded agreeable to Odette. She would further her needlepoint and ponder more on this new Mr. Wardlow.

Hours passed in the most pleasant of thoughts. Then the butler announced, "Mrs. Fenningway, Miss Fenningway, and Miss Eliza."

Odette and her grandmother turned from their seat, sharing a settee and smiled. Odette's was the kind of smile that felt forced, but was perhaps still presentable. Her grandmother's resembled more a grimace. They stood and curtseyed together.

Grandmother lifted a hand. "Please, come in. We shall ask for some tea."

The butler dipped his head, and Odette knew tea would be arriving any moment.

The ladies curtseyed low and then glided into the room.

As soon as Mrs. Fenningway sat, she fanned herself in great exaggeration. "You will never guess our news."

Neither she nor Grandmother ventured a guess, both apparently believing they would be unsuccessful.

"The marquis has returned." Mrs. Fenningway sat back, her smile growing, awaiting their reaction.

"What wonderful news." Grandmother nodded. "Perhaps here for the holidays?"

"Who can say. Who can say that he is not here to find himself a *wife*?" She pointed to the air for emphasis. "Heaven knows he needs to settle down and find a woman to help manage his place in society, here and in Town."

Odette studied the Fenningway daughters. They sat with pristine posture and blank expressions. She tried to imagine one of them as Lady Wilmington.

"Have you yet seen him?" Odette directed her question to the nearest Fenningway, Miss Eliza.

She clasped and unclasped her hands. "We have not. When we stopped by, we were offered a tour of the house."

"Oh?" Grandmother pursed her lips. "Then perhaps he has not returned."

"He was seen." Mrs. Fenningway jabbed her own lap with a pointy finger. "Two times yesterday."

"Well, Mother, I for one cannot be pleased with him, not when he has been absent all these years." Miss Eliza frowned.

Odette's ears perked up a bit more. Perhaps she would learn more about him. Why had he been missing?

"Who can say why he was? We know nothing about him, Eliza, please. Be respectful."

Miss Eliza pressed her lips together, but then seemed to not be able to contain her thoughts. "And missed his mother's funeral? I hear he has also been dreadfully neglectful to the dealings of our town. Hasn't donated a goose to the poor in all these years."

"His tenants are pleased, and his servants." Grandmother offered her own defense. It was no secret that she had fond feelings for the man when he was a lad.

Mrs. Fenningway leaned forward with her finger ready to jab again. "And whatever you might think of him, he is highly titled and, I hear, successful in his ventures. He has become quite wealthy." Her eyes gleamed.

How could she possibly know that? Odette was quite intrigued by the intruding tendrils of gossip. Their reach was much more invasive than many realized. How unfortunate to be so talked of.

Though she had little respect for those who spread negativity, she couldn't help but be influenced, as she, too, had had similar thoughts. What kind of man neglected his home and family to such a degree?

"I heard he is cruel to animals." Miss Fenningway sniffed. "And children."

Odette almost laughed. And then her grandmother did.

Grandmother wiped her eyes. "Oh, my dear. He can be nothing of the sort. For don't we all know the previous marquis and his wife, may they rest in peace? How could people so dear raise a monster?"

Mrs. Fenningway nodded. "And knowing he is to be wealthy and has hopefully returned for good, he is an excellent candidate for any of you three to marry. So you had best find some good things to think of in regards to him."

Miss Eliza clasped her hands together. "I might like him better if he would receive callers."

Odette tried to imagine such a man—old, uncaring. She almost shook her head. She could not believe there was much to admire in him. Did women marry men they did not admire? Was it too much to ask to respect one's husband? Perhaps she would share with her grandmother how desperately she wished to respect the man she married. She even harbored a secret hope that she could love him, as her parents appeared to have loved each other.

When at last the trio had left them in peace, Grandmother was too tired even for supper. She asked for a tray to be sent to her room. Finally, the topic of the now-dreaded marquis had left with the Fenningways.

Odette was left to once again ponder on the novelty of Mr. Wardlow.

DEAR EUOTA

Cheshire County, England

December 1, 1815

My dearest Euota,

Can you believe, here I am, Amelie Goodson, your dearest friend, writing at Christmas time instead of sitting, gathered in our parlor together? I can hardly believe it myself.

It has taken the greatest chill here in Cheshire of a sudden, and I feel the ache in my bones. But I refuse to be disheartened. How could I be? Especially when I remember how we weathered so much worse in our thin gowns, all in the pursuit of happiness in marriage. Or so it seemed to us. I do believe our parents were after security above all in marriage. Perhaps also happiness if it happened to coincide with security. Do you ever wonder what would have happened to each of us were we to have pursued marriage for love only? Do you ever think about those handsome soldiers we danced with until the late hours? Not a single one with a fortune to his name, but every one more handsome than the next. I believe three of them were quite taken with us.

Goodness, I haven't thought of them in years.

It is Odette's fault for my wandering thoughts. Marrying off that girl is going to be a chore indeed. She sees things so differently. Here I sit attempting to pen exactly how she is, and I hear your voice in my head saying that she is so much like I was. You'd think I'd have more patience, knowing so. But instead, I wish her to avoid all the pitfalls I myself narrowly missed despite my misguided thoughts.

Happy, I am, to hear of your plans for Miss Juliana. Your goddaughter is such a deserving soul, and you are just the one to assist her.

How often I have thought about your and dear Raynald's meeting and laughed myself to tears. If someone can meet and fall in love because of your endearing clumsiness, then anyone can fall. And that is my dearest hope for Odette.

As you know from all the past letters, I have as yet to hear even an inkling of interest from her in traveling to London. I offer her a Season! Gowns. All the enjoyments. But perhaps she already senses what you and I know: that the Season is not for the faint of heart. And one must be incredibly savvy to withstand the other influences there.

Which reminds me. You will never guess who lives near me. Have I yet to tell you? The Knickersons! All three. They are now widowed as well, and living together, and I will have to tell you, much the same personalities. But they've come upon hard times. The eldest never married. And so I ask myself. Do I maintain my grudge against Rose for spilling wine on my new dress at the very moment when I would have been introduced to His Grace? Or do I let such a paltry thing go after all these years? After all, I married well. I led a happy family life.

I never did meet the duke.

Perhaps I shall maintain my grudge a little longer.

My Odette is a dear and visits them often, bringing baskets from the house. That is sufficient, I should say. And selfishly, I'm happy when she brings back news from all the families. As yes, you can imagine I'm certain, that the three of them contain all of Cheshire County's gossip under one roof.

What more can I say except please come swiftly to visit? We would adore shared conversation, and the walks here are only to be loved. Your Julianne might enjoy them above all. I pray your holidays will be as festive as ever. Ours look to be full of neighbors and parties and dinners with those we've known many years. Since our family is very limited, mostly to each other, Odette and I are quite content with dear friends who feel much like family.

I have heard a bit of news. I don't know if it's true. I'll not allow myself to become overly excited to hear such vague gossip, but it is indeed possible that the Marquis of Wilmington has returned. Do you remember my talk of a marquis who inherited, went to Oxford, and we never heard from him again? Yes, the very one is rumored to have returned, although no one has seen him. I know I sound addled. I promise I maintain full use of my intellect, to my knowledge, but what I tell you is true. Word has it he is here. And my old hopes for he and Odette to make something of a match is rekindling, ever so slowly. Perhaps a Season in London might not be needed.

Please write at your earliest convenience. You can imagine I long for our particular type of conversation, that only friends who've been as long acquainted as we can share.

Yours ever,
Amelie

CHAPTER 2

*H*enry smiled at odd intervals, sometimes at his steward, and sometimes off into space; sometimes he smiled at the numbers themselves.

Mr. Hansen likely thought him addled, or perhaps just supremely odd.

Of course, he would blame Miss Odette Goodson. Even her name was something to smile about. She appeared at the oddest times in his thoughts, and what could he do but smile? The turn of her chin, the curl in her hair, the deep coal of her eyes. Even her name was lovely. Granted, she was the first woman who wasn't a servant and under the age of fifty that he'd seen since his return, but she seemed quite a remarkable woman, indeed. And the Goodsons were some of the finest folks in all of Cheshire County.

Mr. Hansen cleared his throat. He had placed a new document in front of Henry and was apparently waiting for a response. "If you wish to read it through and then sign, we can start the investment of funds as you described."

"I'm the most woolgathering woolgatherer of our acquaintance today, aren't I?" He smiled.

Mr. Hansen's stern face softened. "I realize that all this information is enough to make even the most dedicated numbers man cross his eyes."

"It isn't even that. It's more a personal problem, I'm afraid."

"Well, my lord, I cannot help you with those."

"Oh, but you might. You see, I met this woman."

Mr. Hansen hummed and began packing up his stacks of paperwork.

"And she is lovely, quite the most intriguing woman of my acquaintance. Lives here in Cheshire County."

"Hmm."

"And has no idea who I am."

The steward paused. "How can that be? Is she the type to totally isolate?"

"I don't know. She has been away at school. I told her my name. Said I'd been gone for a time. The whole row of her own tenant families all knew me on sight, but this woman . . . didn't ring the slightest bell, no hint of recognition. In fact"—he frowned—"I suspect she might think me rather common."

Mr. Hansen snorted. "Then she is a simpleton indeed."

"No, say no more about her. For she is only uninformed. She said herself she's not one prone to gossip."

"Or I'd say, not prone to listening." Mr. Hansen shook his head and then hefted his large and bulging case. "Shall I return tomorrow?"

"Yes." Henry ran a hand over his face. "We must get through last year's books and then plan for next. Then you shall plague me no more with your rows and rows of debits and credits."

"Very well, my lord." The man nodded and then showed himself out of Henry's office.

The quiet descended with an unwelcome heaviness.

Henry stood. The large windows in his study looked out on the back lawns, the very place where he'd learned cricket and shuttlecock and even how to fish. Their pond was always amply stocked, and the servants were tasked with throwing feed at the fish to keep them biting. He couldn't see the view without thinking of his father. A most excellent man, taken too soon while Henry was at Eton. Too well he remembered the headmaster calling him into his office, an express from the shaky hand of his mother, and the news that he'd lost the man he most loved.

He closed his eyes against the memory that still tugged at him after all these years.

Then to have his mother, too, taken while he was away. This time, the news arrived late, much too late to see her buried, even. Her tombstone mocked his absence.

The Missing Marquis. Isn't that what they called him? His hands fisted. He'd stayed away as long as he could, but at the news of his mother's passing, he knew it was time.

The East Indies could hide a lot of lost souls, but it couldn't make them disappear. And as much as Henry wished to disappear, it was time to take his place in this town. He was the highest-ranking noble, technically the magistrate, and would have been well respected simply as his father's son. They had a responsibility to the good people who lived in Chester, Cheshire County—a responsibility he now meant to fulfill.

His smile returned, thinking about the Goodsons' tenants. He'd spent many a hot afternoon helping old Mr. Goodson before he died, patching tenant roofing. As a young lad, Father had considered this type of service to the neighbors a healthy part of his training. He'd never begrudged the work, though he'd often have preferred a swim in the pond, as most lads might. Especially after his time in the East Indies, he was certain that the time aiding the Goodsons was well spent.

Many nobles would find him eccentric. Some in the town quite likely had. But now, known only as the Missing Marquis to many, they certainly found him even more odd.

And there was nothing for it but for him to finally take his place, pay some visits to the local families, and perhaps even find a wife, a hostess, a woman to help look after his duties at home.

Tinsdale rapped on the door to his study. Henry knew it was him because the man always had the same knock. Two raps, a pause, and then another rap.

"Enter."

"You have guests. A Mrs. Fenningway, a Miss Fenningway, and a Miss Eliza."

"Who?"

But before his good, dutiful butler could repeat the list, Henry held up his hand. "Do I know these ladies?"

"You do not. But your parents were reasonably acquainted. They received them from time to time during calling hours, mostly when there was news or something afoot here."

"Ah, I see. And they have, by chance, heard of my return."

"Most certainly. They would not come call otherwise. This is their second visit. And if I might make an observation, once they see you, the entire town shall be made aware."

"Ah, yes, very good." He considered the butler a minute more. "And the Goodsons?"

If he noticed the abrupt change in subject, Tinsdale gave no indication. "Yes, they are neighbors as well, as their estate abuts ours, and if you recall, we have spent much more time with that couple."

"Were they friends of my parents?"

"They were, yes. Dear friends until your parents were taken from us as well, may they rest in peace." He waited. But when Henry said nothing further, he added, "If it aids in your decision, I did not disclose whether or not you were in the house. I merely suggested I would check with the housekeeper to see if we were offering tours. Their last tour included only the main floor but had not ventured in to the library or the grounds."

Henry's smile grew, and he chuckled. "You are a veritable

genius. So, if I desired, I could continue on as though no one is certain yet that I have returned."

"Precisely. If you so desire."

"I believe I do desire. Thank you, Tinsdale. If you could do the honors of asking Mrs. Taylor to give them a tour, I will stop by the kitchen for a basket for the Knickersons and make a speedy delivery myself."

"Very good, my lord. If you would like, I will give you a few moments before I inform the guests."

"Thank you. You know, you are quite good at what you do."

"Thank you, my lord. Your father always thought so."

Henry nodded, suddenly caught up in missing him and his mother again.

"They spoke so well of you whenever you were away." That was the first mention one of the servants had made of his long absence. Eton, of course, was expected, and his years at Oxford, too, but no one expected the new marquis to leave after Oxford for another continent and not return. And Henry appreciated their discretion. But it was also nice to know that he'd not caused his parents too much frustration. He'd written his mother often, but asked her to keep his dealings a secret.

And he'd been successful.

Their family debts had been taken care of. And they had a growing and thriving business in the East Indies.

He attempted to find the good in his long time away, but he was hard-pressed to find a good enough reason to miss his mother's death.

She wasn't supposed to die, of course. She had been as healthy as ever, as she herself penned in her last letter. But who could predict the onset of fevers?

He cleared his throat, and hopefully his woolgathering. "Thank you, Tinsdale. I will always appreciate all memories of my parents."

Long after Tinsdale had left him to his musings, Henry stood staring out the window.

CHAPTER 3

*A*lthough it seemed as though the whole of her night and all her dreams were spent trying to take Mr. Wardlow's measure, by morning, Odette was no closer to understanding who or what this Mr. Wardlow was than when she fell asleep. But no matter. She would likely never see him again.

Today was the day to deliver tenant baskets and then to go into town to see the Knickerson family.

They were recently hit by hard times, and everyone knew they must rely on the goodness of others. A gentleman's family hit by hard times was often hard-pressed to find means to subsist. She typically felt much more value in serving the tenants, who by all appearances had very little. But the Knickersons were different. Three older ladies, sisters, who had come upon harder times later in life. One never married, and the other two left widows. When the final husband passed away, he'd left them a cottage, but nothing from the estate.

Odette enjoyed them immensely. And they were around the same age as her grandmother, who knew them from her first Season; she'd often grumbled their names in those memories. Apparently, they were not much different then as now, gossiping like crazy, supposing things they weren't meant to suppose, and spreading good and ill will interchangeably as long as it qualified as news.

But Odette found them delightful and harmless, as no one took what they said with any degree of seriousness.

As soon as she delivered the last tenant basket, thinking of Mr. Wardlow all the while, still wondering about his exuberant relationship with these families, her carriage turned toward the Knickerson cottage.

And who did she see up on the roof? The very man himself. A well-dressed Mr. Wardlow. With a tool chest and a hammer, pounding about on the roof.

Not quite able to take her eyes off the sight, she found her way to the front door at the same moment their butler opened it.

Bless the man, he was ancient, and threadbare himself. But he stood as stately as seemed possible for him. He even managed the austere expression most butlers seemed to manage. "Whom shall I say is calling?"

"Miss Goodson, if you please."

"Very good, miss. They are expecting you in the front parlor."

"Thank you." She lifted her basket. "Shall I send this to the kitchen or perhaps we might use the items for tea?"

"Perhaps Miss Knickerson will want to see your kindness before it is sent to the kitchen?" His eyes were alert, and full of gratitude.

She smiled. "Excellent."

A rumbling scraping sounded above them, followed by a sliding, and then the whole of a tool kit fell to the ground behind her.

Odette jumped and placed a hand at her chest. "Goodness."

"Yes." The butler said nothing more, but held his hand out, indicating the location of the parlor, which Odette was very familiar with.

After a few steps, she entered the room.

Miss Rose Knickerson, Agnes Smith, and Harriet Thompson stood as Odette crossed into their small parlor. They stood tall, seemed elegant, and for a moment, Odette wished to be as respectable at an advanced age.

Miss Knickerson waved her in. "Come in, my dear. And tell us all about that grandmother of yours."

They always wanted to hear news of Grandmother. They were friends from their Season—at least these three thought they were friends. Her grandmother seemed to feel less warmly. But all the same, she asked for news of them and seemed pleased that Odette had taken an interest in them, and when she knew Odette was visiting, made sure she had extra food for the three.

"She is well. She sends her greetings." Odette lowered the basket to a near table. "And her favorite tarts."

"Oh, she is lovely. Thank you." Mrs. Smith stood. "Shall we share in our feast with you? Join us for tea."

"Of course, thank you. But I shall save the tarts for you."

They unpacked clotted cream and the tarts and fruits that Odette had brought, each exclaiming over the most-favored gifts. Odette smiled all the while.

Then a servant brought in the tea. Odette was relieved they still seemed to have a staff, limited though it might be.

"Would you pour?" Miss Knickerson's smile was broad and friendly. She was the jolliest of the three.

"And don't spill this time, mind." Mrs. Thompson tended to have the sharpest tongue. Odette imagined her reprimands could be quite stern, but she paid her little mind.

"Oh tosh, Harriet. Odette has never spilled a drop of tea while she is here."

"There's always a first time. Sometimes a reminder does wonders for these young lasses."

"Pay her no mind." Mrs. Smith shook her head. "You may

pour the tea as you wish, and even spill a drop or two if you like."

Mrs. Thompson's frown deepened.

"Have no fear. I shall not spill. Though I cannot guarantee a perpetually steady hand, I have not had trouble with tea as of yet."

"You see, Harriet? She'll be just fine."

Odette could only laugh inside at these women and their conversations. "How are the ducks in your pond?"

"Oh, there's that one mallard. He's a menace if I've ever seen one." Mrs. Thompson bit into a tart as though it was a chore.

"What is the mallard up to now?" Odette watched them over her cup, grinning into her tea.

"Oh, they're all just delightful." Mrs. Smith waved her hand. "They would love more visitors. Sometimes we get the children coming to feed our birds. Perhaps you'd like to do the same?"

"That sounds lovely. Perhaps I shall." She suspected the children in the schoolroom might like the diversion, and the Knickersons would certainly be delighted with more visitors for their ducks. She would stop by this week to share as much with the schoolmaster.

Something fell from the sky outside the window.

"What was that?" Miss Knickerson craned her neck to see more of the window.

The other two giggled.

"What is it?" Odette knew it was likely Mr. Wardlow dropping something or other again. But after the whole of his toolbox fell, he couldn't have much else, could he?

But then he stood up, himself, outside the window.

Odette jumped up. "Goodness!"

The other ladies squealed, and the butler stepped into the room. "Might I be of assistance?" His typically stoic expression reigned, but Odette saw the slightest twitch of his lip, indicating perhaps a certain concern.

"Our lad, Henry, just fell from the roof." Miss Knickerson pointed to Mr. Wardlow, who was brushing off his jacket and seemed to be otherwise perfectly fine.

"Yes, it appears he is having a difficult time of things. But he did bid me mention that the hole has been mended."

"See, what a dear boy he is. A local chap. Just as dear as when his father brought him round when he was a young chap, I'm certain, though I cannot remember. Was it he who came round? Or perhaps it was that Tucker boy. Did we live here as children? Did you tell him to join us?"

"I did indicate as you directed, that he was welcome, but he said he was going to walk the fence line to see if it needs mending."

The ladies did everything but fan themselves in exuberance over Mr. Wardlow and his attention. And all Odette could do was puzzle some more.

Mrs. Smith leaned forward. "Now you, Miss Goodson."

Odette swallowed her fruit. "Yes, Mrs. Smith?"

"You are of the age to start thinking about marrying."

Odette breathed deeply, attempting to maintain her good posture. "Yes, Grandmother has been saying much the same."

"She is a wise woman. Our times during the Season were a prime example of how a woman can never be too careful nor too lax in her pursuit of marriage." Mrs. Smith clucked. "We can attest that good marriages are available for all the deserving women of the ton." She rested a hand on Miss Knickerson's. "And we equally assert that the very best of us at times are not so blessed."

Mrs. Thompson sniffed. "Certainly for those who do not attempt to entrap a man."

Miss Knickerson nodded. "And I would never degrade myself in such a manner."

They talked more, breathing out heated memories from their Season of all the women who had married men of title. Apparently, it was a great year of entrapment as a method of marriage. And Odette could do nothing more but listen and wonder after Mr. Wardlow.

At last, they'd eaten their fill from the basket, and she'd drunk her fill of tea. She stood. "I must be going. Thank you for your kind attention."

"Oh, do come back, my dear. Please tell Amelie that we hope she is well," Miss Knickerson said.

"I will, thank you." She curtseyed.

Their butler showed up like magic to open the front door. "Thank you," she murmured on the way out. One might as well thank the servants, she'd always thought.

"Our other guest"—the butler cleared his throat—"mentioned that he would be walking the side of the property if you would care for some exercise." His eyes stared straight ahead, but his lip again made a twitch.

She nodded. "Would you be so kind as to point the direction he went?"

"Certainly." The butler indicated she begin off to the eastern side of the property.

And so she followed.

She told herself she was going because she had been so curious about him. Naturally, she would use the time to take his measure, to figure out once and for all who this man was who had so captivated her attention. She tried not to notice the uptick in her heart. Or the quickened way she was breathing. Perhaps she was not used to walking . . .

CHAPTER 4

*H*enry watched for Miss Goodson, all the while noting any troubles with the fence line.

He wasn't knowledgeable about these things, not really. He barely knew enough about roof repair to make a difference, but their problem was obvious and simple to fix, so he'd made an attempt. The fence might prove much more difficult, but he would send his own servants over to make the repairs. His excuse for walking it at all was that he was hoping to linger, away from the ladies who lived there, in such a way that he might be able to talk more with Miss Goodson.

He rubbed his shoulder then took off his jacket. He was sore from head to toe. That fall might leave its marks. Good thing there was a rather large bush which caught him, and his quick thinking made him roll with his weight when he landed.

All the same, he knew he'd be sitting in a bath tonight for as long as the water would remain warm. He walked as slowly as he dared, not wanting to seem a wastrel, but hoping to remain relatively close to the house. She as yet had not made an appearance. He might give up on Miss Goodson and ride home to calm his tired muscles.

But then the dogs started barking. The Knickersons had all manner of barn animals, except really horses. Their one remaining horse was a decrepit thing that he was half tempted to steal and feed properly. Perhaps he'd send his servants over for that task as well.

The dogs yipped and jumped and ran in circles to such a degree that he knew Miss Goodson would step into view right before she did.

And she was a glorious sight. Her bonnet in hand, the breeze tickling her hair, lifting and toying with the curls at her neckline, fighting against the restraining bun.

Was he so entranced because she was the oasis after the desert? He refused to believe such a thing. He had not wanted to even lay eyes on the Fenningways, who'd come to call just yesterday.

She played with the dogs while making her way toward him. Her face was light, her smile bright. And her laugh was again a trill in his soul as soon as she was close enough for him to hear.

When she at last had joined him, all he could think of to say was, "You came."

She laughed again, which warmed him to his very toes.

"I did."

He nodded twice and fumbled about for words before then offering his arm. "Forgive me. I'm so unaccustomed to such things. Would you care to walk a bit of the fence line with me?"

"I'd like that very much, thank you."

Her hand on his arm felt nice . . . and unsettling in the best manner. They stepped side by side, his long strides adjusting to match her shorter ones.

Now, for a moment to get to know her better. He must discover why this woman had attracted his interest. "Tell me. What do you think of the three Knickerbocks?"

She laughed again. "What an odd thing to call them."

"It is their name, is it not?"

"Knickerson. But not for many years. Two were married, you know. I find them highly amusing. And how do you find them?"

"The same as you. I met them as a lad. At the time, Mr. Knicker*son* was still living. The sisters would visit at times. They're quite energetic, the three of them."

"Yes, they are. My grandmother knew them in London. I think they all came out the same year."

"Really!" He couldn't imagine that the Mrs. Goodson he remembered would get on well with the three in that house. "They *are* an entertaining bunch. Did I see you bring in a basket?"

Her eyes flit up to his, a flash of pleasure lighting her face. "You did. I came with tea and some extras."

"Do you come often?"

"I have been coming once a week, after a visit to the tenants." Her eyes studied him. "The same tenants who seem to know you so well. As do these ladies. How are you so acquainted with everyone?"

He opened his mouth to respond and paused. Did he want her to know he was the marquis? He should. She might be more interested in him if she knew. But did he want this intriguing woman to light up in interest simply because of his title? He knew he did not. Nor did he wish anyone to know of his return. However, it wasn't as though he could keep his identity from her. He frowned.

"Goodness, if it's a secret, you needn't tell me." She removed her hand from his arm.

He felt the loss immediately. "Oh dear, no. Please." He lifted her fingers. "My arm needs the presence of your lovely hand."

Her smile returned.

He tucked her hand into his side on his arm. "I was simply at a loss to explain."

She waited.

"I grew up in the neighborhood. The Wardlows have been here since anyone lived here at all."

She nodded.

"And my father was a socially engaging sort of chap and brought me along with him. I think he felt a sense of responsibility for his neighbors."

"Is that why you were up on the roof?"

"And falling off? Yes." He rotated his shoulders. "I fear I'm not the most qualified to be doing these sorts of tasks, but I well remember my father doing much the same. He would attempt to do all manner of jobs to help at home and with the neighbors, eventually engaging the servants to assist."

Her nose wrinkled in such an adorable expression of confusion that he wished at once to create such a look again. Laughing to himself, he added, "I shall send servants to fix this fence."

"Oh!" Her hand went to her mouth. "Are you a gentleman, then?"

He paused in his steps, then continued. Of course he was a gentleman. Did he not look like one? Act like one? He was immediately plagued with all manner of insecurities. Perhaps his time in the East Indies had robbed him of his deportment. "I certainly try to be." Concern rose inside.

The Knickersons' old horse ran out from the barn toward them. The dogs ran to meet him, barking and leaping. The horse stomped his feet.

"Oh dear." He paused and ran a hand through his hair.

"What's the matter?"

He pointed and allowed his hand to fall at his side. "That horse."

"Will he be trouble?" She lifted eyes to his face, catching him in the full force of her gaze.

Henry swallowed twice before he could think coherently and then nodded. "Most definitely."

They watched while the horse seemed to tolerate the dogs for a moment more and then took off running toward the back end of the property.

Henry sighed.

"What is the matter?" Her confusion had returned.

"That horse won't return unless I drag it back."

"How can you know? Has such a thing occurred?"

"Oh, yes, on more than one occasion since my return." He groaned. "The truth is, the poor animal might be better off fending for itself."

"But the ladies use it for their cart?"

"They do indeed."

They both stared after the running nag for many seconds, and then turned together. "We better get him."

"I'll go after him."

Their words, uttered at the same moment, were spoken with a mixture of resignation and humor.

Henry grinned. "How did you arrive this afternoon?"

"By carriage."

"Oh, pity."

"How so?"

He felt his cheeks warm. "Oh, well, that is perhaps a wonderful way to come. I was just thinking how enjoyable it might have been to chase after the horse together." He laughed. "But instead, I shall walk you to the carriage and then figure out that devil of a horse."

"Oh dear. Yes. I should have loved to assist."

He found he did not particularly wish to be parted from her company. "Perhaps we might go riding sometime?"

"I'd like that, yes."

"Excellent." He nodded. They turned to walk back toward her carriage.

The horse whinnied in the distance.

"Will you go after him?"

"He does seem to be enjoying himself overly much."

"Will he go far?"

"No, fortunately, he often finds himself at my own barn."

Sadly, their visit together was about to end. And at just the right place that allowed Henry to not answer Miss Goodson's question completely, to prevent her from inquiring as to the location of his barn.

Of course, he could not keep such a thing a secret. She would know, and sooner rather than later. But for now, he was enjoying a bit of anonymity, the kind of thing not granted to him very often.

They arrived at her carriage. "And here is where you ride off in comfort while I chase down a sad and sorry horse." He wiggled his eyebrows.

"I do wish you the very best." Her eyes held a new sort of hope that he enjoyed.

"Thank you. And I do hope that too many days do not pass before we two are on our own horses riding, perhaps across Goodson land?"

"Oh, yes. Please come call. We can ride wherever you like."

"Very good." He took her hand and bowed with his most gallant expression, pressing his lips to the back of her glove. "Until then."

"Yes." Did her voice sound breathless?

A look into her face showed a calm expression. Perhaps she was merely speaking quietly. Goodness, he was more interested in her reactions than he'd been in anyone else of his acquaintance. Perhaps with time, he could win over an equal amount of fervor from her.

For now, she seemed to enjoy his company. She was interested in him with the mild curiosity of one meeting a new friend.

And that was simply not good enough.

CHAPTER 5

*O*dette arrived home determined to hear what Grandmother knew of this man.

A quick handoff of her bonnet and gloves at the entry table and a distracted look around the front foyer told her that Grandmother must be up in her sitting room. It was about the time of day she would go sit up there with her books and her art. She'd created a studio for herself in one section of her rooms.

And it was there, brush in hand, where Odette found her.

The bold strokes, the strong colors, the thick textures told Odette that the woman must be deep in thought, and the emotions were high.

"Grandmother?"

"Come in, child." She was staring at her canvas.

"That's striking."

Her lips tugged up into a smile. "I'll agree with you there. This deep purple here, that's because I miss my parents. They came to England with me the very year I was coming out. They gave me a Season in London. They knew." She shook her head. And then she added a bright yellow across the top of her painting. "They knew what France would become." She ran the back

35

of her hand along her forehead. "And that blue there?" She sniffed.

Odette stepped forward to wrap an arm across Grandmother's shoulder. "That blue is my Armand. Who'd have guessed at my brilliant luck that I could marry a man with French blood here in England?" She switched brushes and dipped the next in a muted green. "And this is the strong wind that blew today. I felt it deep in my bones while on a walk this morning."

"Did you walk?"

Her lips twitched. "Yes, I walked."

Odette laughed. "I'm pleased to hear it."

"And where have *you* been walking?"

"Me? Oh, well I . . ."

"Did you deliver the basket to the Knickersons?"

"I did, Grandmother, and they send their greetings and gratitude to you."

"Excellent. I'm pleased you visit them, but remember also that most of what they say is all kinds of rubbish."

"Yes, though they are harmless. Aren't they?"

"No one who carries as much news as they do is harmless. Who's to know if any of that nonsense is even true."

"You're right, Grandmother."

"But they sent me a card while you were there."

"What?"

"Yes, apparently they still have some servants who can walk."

"Oh, I guess so."

"They mentioned that you were out walking, after their visit."

Odette moaned silently, then nodded. "Yes."

"With the man who fixes their roof?"

"He's a gentleman."

Her grandmother's eyebrows rose just as Odette's had. Why would a gentleman behave so? How could he be?

She didn't have an answer to her own questions.

"And you believe that?"

"I hadn't doubted him until now."

"And you were alone."

She sighed, suddenly tired of the conversation. "Do you really think it matters?"

"Certainly. Of all the people in all of Cheshire, those three are the ones you do not want to slip up in front of. They long to share a juicy bit of news. They did as debutantes, and from what I can tell, they are even more hungry for relevant information now."

"Well, I can assure you in every way that we were nothing but appropriate, in full view of anyone the entire time, and merely discussing how to assist the women. Their nag got free and he rode after it." She shrugged. "Which I grant does not sound much like something a gentleman would do, but honestly, perhaps he is more like I am. More the kind to aid and assist and less worried about station." Her voice trailed off. She did not enjoy having to explain anything to her grandmother. She felt as though she'd committed the unpardonable. A sick clenching of her stomach accompanied her thoughts.

"I think we should accept more invitations and begin calling on our neighbors. We have a good group here. There are eligible men. And of course we heard that the marquis himself might have returned."

"The Marquis of Wilmington?" Odette's nose wrinkled. "The very one who deserted his estate and missed his own mother's death?"

"We do not know the particulars. As I said, his servants have been well cared for, his steward excellent."

Odette nodded. "Too true. I am being too harsh." But inside, she could not like him. As the only family of title in their small town, she viewed he had a greater responsibility here in Cheshire and not away. But she acknowledged she did not know. How could she be aware of his reasons and particular situation? "Do we know where he went? Why he left?"

Grandmother shook her head. "Not at all, but he was the finest of lads, the most promising of men when he left for Oxford. That I do know. A person never goes too far from his roots."

Odette wasn't too certain of that, but she kept her thoughts to herself. At least her grandmother was past assuming her own improper behavior.

"And this man, this worker man . . ." Grandmother tsked. "In the very moment that the marquis has arrived, you would risk a situation that could limit your opportunities with him? Perhaps you should resist walking out alone with this stranger, in public or private. If he were a proper gentleman, he would come call at least."

"I do think he might." She wished she could swallow the words back into the depths of her mouth as she said them. What if he did not? And what if, when he did, Grandmother did not approve?

Grandmother frowned. "We shall see if we can learn more about him then." Her voice said she highly doubted she would be impressed.

"Very well." Odette now wished for some time alone in her own rooms.

But Grandmother had other plans. "Let's discuss a Season in London."

Odette pulled out her needlework and moved to sit beside her grandmother. "Why do you wish it so?"

"I was hoping that you, too, would wish it. A Season in London is every young woman's dream."

"Was it yours?"

She paused, and then sighed a sort of exasperated sound. "Not really."

Odette laughed. "Why not?"

"I wished to have a Season, of course. I wanted to marry and to be happy. I wanted to be a success more than anything." She adjusted her skirts, avoiding the question entirely.

"And were you?"

"I was happy. I am happy. I married for love. I was blessed to do so. I thought a Season was my dream. But looking back, I see that besides the dear friends I made, the Season was one full of nerves, worry, thinking and pining an overly large amount, and a great amount of unhappiness."

Nothing about a Season was sounding more appealing. Odette paused before asking the most obvious question in the world. "So—"

"Why do I want you to have one?" Grandmother added a streak of green to her painting. "Because it is worth it. No matter how much sorrow for the ridiculousness of others the Season will bring, you can gain what is most desired. And because I will not be around forever. And we don't have anyone but each other." She turned tender eyes to Odette, so tender, she almost teared up herself. She loved her grandmother.

"I could not bear to leave this earth knowing you were uncared for."

Odette stood and wrapped her arms around Grandmother's shoulders. "And you shan't. I promise." She sniffed. "I don't really wish to be alone either, you know."

"Yes, I know." Grandmother patted her hand. "We will do our best to see you situated. And I know you can't see it right now, but we just might find who you're looking for right here in Cheshire County."

She thought immediately of Mr. Wardlow. Just as she knew her grandmother was thinking of that marquis. If she was going to think well of Mr. Wardlow or give him any sort of attention, she knew she had best convince her grandmother that he was an appropriate acquaintance, at the very least. She best do so quickly, at least before this marquis at last made an appearance.

Mr. Wardlow had said he would come call and that they would ride. That would be the first opportunity. With any luck, he knew how to come call—hopefully, he would have pristine manners and come from a good family. She, too, was looking forward to hearing his answers to some of the questions she knew her grandmother would ask.

Until then, she would need to put him out of her mind. She couldn't be having fanciful thoughts about a man who might very well be wholly inappropriate for her.

CHAPTER 6

*H*enry received multiple letters regarding his ships that very afternoon. Things were moving forward as planned. There were some questions about a captain for his newest ship. These East Indiaman were aptly named: a ship to go from England to the East Indies and back, over and over. He was consumed by the planning and making early decisions about cargo. Days went by before Henry was able to even schedule a time to see Miss Goodson. And by then, the weather had taken an even more icy chill. So much so that the pond at the back of his property had frozen over.

With that diversion in mind, he made his way over to the Goodson house. They lived on one of the most beautiful properties in all of Cheshire County, in Henry's opinion. They boasted two streams and the tallest and grandest pines. The hills rolled about them in every direction. He had always loved walking their land and had been grateful that the late Mr. Goodson seemed not to mind at all even when he was a young lad and could have caused trouble. He grinned. In fact, Mr. Goodson had helped him catch his first fish.

The ground crunched beneath his feet. Servants had placed

two sets of ice skates under the bench in his carriage for him. He was unaccountably exuberant to be able to spend some time with Miss Goodson. He hadn't planned to stay much longer in Cheshire County than the length of a good, cold winter. Then he'd be off to London. His whole fleet might be at the docks there before he was able to arrive himself.

Although his mind was very much engaged and his heart longed to be with his new fleet, the unexpected diversion of the beautiful Miss Goodson kept him sufficiently entertained and very much distracted.

As he approached her front door, movement through the front room window caught his eye. Miss Goodson, on the pianoforte. But she'd apparently seen him and stopped playing. Her hand raised in a greeting, and she stood.

He lifted his hand to the knocker.

Their butler opened the door, with Miss Goodson right behind.

"Please come in." The servant's mildly amused tone was not lost on Henry, who held out his arm and then escorted Miss Goodson to her own front room.

"And how are you this afternoon?" he asked.

"I'm well. I'm so pleased you have come. Though Grand-mother will be terribly disappointed to have missed you."

"Oh? Has she been counting the moments until I arrive?"

"No. It's not quite like that." Her cheeks colored just enough that Henry wondered precisely how it was.

"Well, I am equally disappointed to have missed her. Please give her my regards."

"Certainly. Thank you."

"In fact, since she is unavailable, perhaps we might ask for some warm outer-clothing for you and leave posthaste?"

"And what do you have in mind?" Her bright smile rewarded him with a spreading warmth and happiness.

"Ice skating?"

"Oh yes!" She clapped her hands once and held them to her chest. "I haven't been in years, and I've been hoping it would get cold enough. Do you think the ice will be thick enough?"

"I do. I tested it myself to be certain."

She looked aptly impressed with his preparation. And so he turned them about and waited in the foyer while she was outfitted for the colder weather.

She descended the stairs in a lovely red coat, with mittens and a warm-looking fur hat.

"You look perfectly lovely."

"Thank you. At least I shall be warm."

"Certainly."

Her maid joined them, which he found cumbersome, but her presence reminded him of the general propriety of the ton and that he should be very careful in his behavior. If the cold weather didn't remind him, the presence of her maid did. He was not in the East Indies any longer.

He helped them both up into his carriage, and he sat as close as he dared to Miss Goodson. "I wonder if you have skated much?"

"Oh, all winter long if I can. I admit to sneaking onto the marquis's property to use his pond."

"The very place we will be going today."

"As long as he doesn't see us, I suppose."

Henry opened his mouth and then closed it. As he suspected, she still had no idea who he was, but to hear she had a less than stellar opinion of him was a bit disconcerting to say the least. "And why would that be such a terrible thing?"

She huffed out a large breath and then, to his surprise, frowned. "I just don't imagine a man who has neglected his duty for so long would be the sort to be generous."

He could say nothing to that. He'd certainly neglected his duty. He'd missed his own mother's funeral. She was correct in her assessment. Another voice reminded him that by being away, he'd also done much good for the estate and increased their wealth fourfold. But that voice was smaller, and in the face of Miss Goodson's firm disapproval, he could only agree. "I have it on good authority that we will be undisturbed."

She nodded. "Our properties abut."

"Yes, you have the lovelier of the two."

"Oh, I don't know. I do admire the marquis's shrubs, and his pines are closer together in places. And of course, the pond. He also has this walk on the west side of his property, through the rose gardens." Her smile was blissful. "I feel almost guilty that I am one of few to enjoy the beauty."

Henry dipped his head, pleased that she would admire his property at the same time that she apparently disapproved of himself. He'd have to remedy that somehow. And he wasn't at all certain how to explain who he was, now that she'd said those things. She'd feel awkward and uncertain around him if he let her know today. But certainly, he couldn't leave her feeling negative about him.

They arrived at the pond, and as requested, a table was set with tea.

"Oh dear. It looks as though he is entertaining."

"Or I am." He smiled.

Her eyes widened. "You did this?"

"I did."

"Thank you." She reached for his hand as he helped her down out of the carriage.

"Our skates are just inside."

A footman retrieved them and then set about placing chairs and blankets and further creating the festive atmosphere he was hoping for.

When at last their skates were on, they hobbled closer to the edge of the pond and then stepped out onto the ice.

"Shall we do a few laps to warm up?" he asked.

"Excellent. What are we warming up for?"

"For the most excellent tricks and competitions we shall endeavor to impress each other with."

She laughed again. "Oh, I don't know if you can be as impressive as I."

"Excellent. Are you competitive, then?"

"I might be, depending on the situation." She raised an eyebrow in such a challenging expression, he was determined to see her do so again. He laughed heartily.

But her hand was on his arm, and she used him to steady herself enough that he kept the pace slow, and they circled many times. "Tell me more about growing up here in Cheshire," he said.

"Oh, well, I wasn't born here. I spent the first ten years of my life by the sea in Brighton."

"I love the sea."

"Do you?"

"Very much so. I particularly love being out on it, on a great ship, with water all around in every direction."

Miss Goodson shivered.

"Are you cold?"

"No." She laughed. "That was more of a shiver of enjoyment." She looked away, obviously feeling self-conscious.

"I love that."

"You do?"

"Certainly. And I wonder. Have you ever *been* out on a ship in the middle of the ocean?"

"I have not. I long to do so, but where would I go? Why would I do such a thing? My grandmother and I live a simple life."

"Do you wish to travel?"

"I don't think so? Although, the way you describe the sea sounds appealing. I remember standing on the beach at Brighton, watching the waves come in, wondering where they begin."

He shook his head. "And that's the very beauty of the ocean.

They don't begin. They just always . . . are. The water rolls on forever in soft swells. Unless it is full of tempest, and then the waves rage in sharp peaks, sending the boat towards the heavens and then down towards the depths. I cannot account for it."

"But how can a thing never begin?" Her nose wrinkled, and he wished to tap it with his finger.

"That I do not know, but perhaps that is how our world is? How did it begin? The tiniest grain of sand, how did it get here? The sky, when did it appear?" He grinned up into the sky. Soft flakes had begun to fall. "And where do these come from?"

"You are a deep thinker."

"As are you if you're wondering where the waves come from."

"I suppose I am."

"So if you arrived in Cheshire at the age of ten, then I missed you by a hair, for I was off to Eton."

"You attended Eton?" Her tone of surprise was amusing.

"Yes, and then Oxford. I'm afraid I've spent little time here."

"But you grew up here?"

"I did up until the age of twelve, when I left for Eton, as I said." He sighed. "I missed the dear place for the first few years, and then it began to feel less and less like home."

"Grandmother wishes for me to go to London."

He approved of her going to London, as it was the very place he planned to live while organizing his East Indiaman ships. "And you don't wish to yourself?"

"I just don't want to have a Season there. I don't want to be on display, vying for attention, attempting to win a husband." Her soft gasp and the hand that soon covered her mouth was endearing. He pretended not to notice her dismay, but she laughed it off. "I should not have shared something so personal. Tell me of Oxford. What did you study?"

"I would love to speak of Oxford. Though husband hunting seems much more entertaining." Henry smiled as she gasped softly again, then repented of his tease. "Some of the happiest times of my life were spent at Oxford. But first, I must emphasize, I enjoy all the words you share—every glimpse to know you better has become quite fascinating to me. I cannot explain it, but there you have it, and so please, whatever you wish to express, I am all ears to hear you."

She nodded and looked away. They did not know each other well enough. And how could he share more with her, things that might reveal he was the marquis she so detested? Perhaps he could change her mind.

"I was surprised at your chagrin about our unwitting host today."

"Were you?"

"Yes, he does seem an amiable chap, by all accounts." Henry held his breath. Perhaps she could be swayed.

"I've heard nothing of him; no one seems to know him. No one has seen him here at all for the whole of their lives." She snorted. "The only people I know of who speak his name are seeking his hand." She colored again. "Forgive me. I am so bold. I don't know what it is about our time together, but I say things I shouldn't. And here you will now think me a gossip, akin to the sisters we visited last week."

"No. Saints preserve you. Say such things no more."

"You are kind. But I'm pleased at least the Marquis is amiable."

There, a slight improvement perhaps in her impression of him.

"And now, I believe we are steady on our skates. Perhaps I can show you a trick or two?" He pressed her hand beneath his on his arm once before skating ahead. When he reached a sufficient distance, he spun. "You see?! I've become proficient."

"Most excellent." She clapped, but she did not look overly impressed.

"Can you do the same?"

"I believe so." She nodded, then skated with her arms out, as gracefully as a dancer might. She picked up speed and then spun in two circles.

"Ho ho! Besting me already, are you?"

"Have I?" She grinned.

"You know you have." He spun halfway. "Can you go backwards?"

She approached, grasping onto his outstretched hands while he skated back.

"How are you managing such a thing?"

He concentrated on moving his feet, then pulled her closer. "Perhaps I can manage better if you make certain we don't crash into the bank?"

"I can do that." Was her voice breathless now? A bit? Her cheeks were colored again, but perhaps from the exertion.

He held her close. She gripped his arms, and kept her eyes focused on the ice to their front.

"This is a bit like dancing."

"It is." She looked up into his face, and her eyes shone. "I do enjoy dancing."

"Does Cheshire have many balls?"

"Not a one lately. I do hope that some of the larger homes will consider a Twelfth Night Ball, or some such during the holidays."

And right then, he decided. He would host a ball. A dinner and a ball. Two events more than he'd ever hosted in his life. But she helped him see his duty to the neighborhood. And he admitted, he'd do much to be able to hold her again such as he was. Would he win her approval of the marquis? He had to. Because suddenly, what he wanted most out of Cheshire was the winning smile of a certain Miss Goodson.

CHAPTER 7

*B*oxing Day. She could do much to celebrate their servants on Boxing Day. The ideas just started flowing. Odette had been attempting to consider what more she could do for the families in their area, and she decided that perhaps they could broaden the Boxing Day celebrations to include tenants as well as servants. They could have a celebration in the center of town, near the fountain. Perhaps even decorate a tree there like the queen was known to do. She couldn't possibly give gifts to everyone, not in addition to the baskets of food and things she would deliver, but perhaps they could be encouraged to swap gifts themselves? Or they could have a celebration of music and dancing.

The idea filled her with magic. And, she realized, soothed a loneliness that came over her every Christmas time. She loved her grandmother, as much as her own parents, but she longed for larger groups of people. She dreamed of a family filling a room, celebrating together. And so she went in search of her grandmother with her notes and a quill in hand.

But apparently her grandmother was also very active with plans of her own. She sat with a correspondence in hand and her own quill scratching across the page. "I have excellent news. Come in, sit. Let me finish this letter and I shall share all."

As soon as she finished, Odette asked, "Who are you writing?"

"Euota. She sends her love. Did you know she was one of my dear friends from our Season in London? I hold each of them dear, like a sister. The Season is not just about marrying, you know."

"I'm happy you have such dear friends. They're like aunts to me, certainly."

"They were the best kind then, and loyal in their correspondence now. Each married and has led a life full of triumphs and challenges." She lifted a stack of four letters, sealed with her signature wax. "Margarette Fudge, Euota Savile, Temperance Bolingbroke, and Esther Langdon. I'm sending them a bit of ribbon and a bell."

Odette watched Grandmother's eyes mist over and felt a pang of longing for such an experience herself. For the first time, a Season in London seemed like something more than a chore. She still did not wish to go, but now at least she saw a higher potential.

"I have recently learned that the marquis himself has let rooms in Town."

"The marquis? Our marquis?"

Grandmother's eyes twinkled. "I hope one day to make him *our marquis,* if that's what you mean. Yes, the very one who has an estate abutting ours. The one whom I've wished for all these years that you could meet. He was a dear lad. He is surely a good man. And you could have your wish, to live here."

"But he's letting rooms in Town?"

She nodded, blissfully securing another sheaf of parchment. "And I suspect he hopes to buy a home in Town." She dipped her quill. "I am writing to accept Euota's invitation for the two of us to go and stay this spring, late winter even. I do believe they would welcome us as soon as Twelfth Night has been celebrated." She sniffed. "And they are so highly connected. Oh, my dear Odette, this is all I've ever hoped for you."

She opened her mouth to speak, as a response was likely needed, but she didn't have anything to say. Her grandmother seemed positively giddy.

"Thank you, Grandmother."

The woman looked up, and then tsked. "Come, child. You are unhappy? Please see the good in this. Who is here in Cheshire for you? Even the marquis is off to London. If you cannot see it now, you must trust me. I have your happiness in mind."

"I believe you, Grandmother. And I trust you. But I have never been to London, and I have a hard time believing I will enjoy it more than my home that I love." Should she mention Mr. Wardlow? She wanted to. Something stayed her tongue. She knew her grandmother would be displeased she'd seen him again without him coming calling to visit her. But he'd tried. Grandmother would have to give him that, though Odette felt certain the woman's heart was set against this stranger.

And who was he really? She still had much to puzzle over where he was concerned. But even the thought of him was bringing a lovely rush of warmth. He had this twinkle about him. Just like the first day she'd ever met him, with his prancing horses, he seemed to carry a certain happiness that always spread to her.

And skating in his arms had been wonderful. He was strong, sure, and close. She smiled.

"See, your smile has returned. I knew you would begin to see London as something to look forward to." Grandmother clucked. "Now, let us enjoy our Christmas festivities."

"Oh!" She sat taller. "I have some thoughts about Boxing Day."

Her grandmother's smile lines deepened. Her voice, soft and clear, smiled at Odette in its tenderness as well. "Thank you, my dear. Someone needs to be thinking more of those kinds of things. I find I grow tired."

"I'm hoping to create something of a larger celebration."

She knew her grandmother tried to hide it, but her tired sigh was plainly audible.

"And I shall not disturb you with the details."

Grandmother's expression turned soft. "I'm pleased you want to do so much good. And your service to the tenants does you credit. But do not overwork yourself. They will enjoy their Christmas well with or without a large celebration."

Odette nodded, unsure what her grandmother was trying to say, but still determined to do something. "I find that I enjoy them. I like the idea of more people surrounding us this season."

"I as well find that encouraging. Perhaps there will be parties, balls, dinners. One can only guess. If everyone returns to Cheshire for December, as they seem to be doing, we just might be in luck."

"Perhaps."

Her grandmother held out her hand. "Come. I'm sorry I have not the large family to give you."

Odette slipped around the desk and wrapped her arms around Grandmother, her throat suddenly full. "Do not be sorry. You have given me everything."

"I do love you, my dear. That you can be sure of."

She nodded. "I know. Thank you, Grandmother."

"Oh, you don't need to be thanking me. You are easy to love."

"And I love you too." She squeezed her grandmother extra tight and then collected her papers and her quill. "Perhaps I shall write in the sitting room this morning?"

"Excellent idea. And your books are likely still there from yesterday."

"True." She curtseyed. "Will we take our walk this afternoon?"

"Oh, I think I'm too tired today. This cold air hurts my bones in a way they've never felt before."

"Would you rather I stayed inside?"

"No, you get your walk in. I know how you love it. And I should very much like to hear about the state of the greenery that is braving all this snow."

"Oh, certainly. I have been watching the particular shrubs, as you know."

Grandmother chuckled and waved her out, then sat back in her seat, staring out her window. In repose, her grandmother looked older than Odette remembered the woman to be.

For the first time in her life, Odette wondered how long she would have the blessing of the old woman's companionship.

DEAR EUOTA

December 12, 1815

My Dear Euota,

I have precious little news to share. My efforts to bring together my dear Odette and the marquis have come to naught up to this point. Though I have heard news. He is letting a home in London, and I didn't tell this to Odette, because she would be opposed to the monetary nature of the conversation, but he has come upon great wealth. His time away was fruitful indeed, and he is building his own fleet of ships.

I do not know if you have sensibilities about trade. But I, for one, see wealth as a great blessing no matter from whence it comes. And he has a title. No one could fault him.

I think I have squelched Odette's talk of a local boy. What could he be to the marquis, whom I know to come from an impeccable family, to be the kindest of lads?

I hope all is well with you.

How are your own plans? Is it not greatly diverting that we are all so caught up in the matchmaking of others?

My bones ache. Odette doesn't know how sharply they

bother. Perhaps I shall call the physician. I suspect it's all because of the cold that has suddenly hit us. I hear even the pond is frozen through. Someone saw a young couple out skating the other day.

But I do admit to enjoying the snow from inside by the fire. Watching it falling in its soft magic, covering the earth with its pure whiteness. There is nothing like it, I tell you. And I fear we will have quite a large snowfall this year, if my aching bones are any indication. As December 24 approaches, I find I am less and less excited about our normal festivities and too tired to encourage the boxes of decorations be unloaded from the attic. Still, I have enclosed a bit of ribbon and a bell, with hopes that you will think of me this season. I know you shall. We've spent so many weeks together this time of year, you can hardly avoid thinking of me. I long for the day we might spend a Christmas together again. This year does feel a bit melancholy without you in it, and the others. But until then, these ornaments will cure some of the doldrums. I spoke to Odette of our friendship today, and that at last seems to have done the trick necessary for her to agree to a Season. She did not necessarily verbalize anything, but the hope in her eyes changed. We will get there. I have my own hope for this match with the marquis. If the match cannot be established here, we shall make the journey to London. But I digress. Who would have thought my every breath would be caught in the plans of a matchmaking biddy? I'm hardly recognizing myself. But I love my dear Odette, and do so wish to see her settled before . . . well, before I am too old to enjoy the celebrations.

All my love,
Amelie .

CHAPTER 8

*H*enry smiled at his valet. "Our ice skating went well."

"Very good, my lord."

"I think that perhaps she might warm to me with time."

"Certainly." The valet brushed down Henry's jacket.

"Do you find it odd that she would be so averse to the marquis?"

"My lord?"

"Yes. She finds me disdainful."

"I don't understand." In a rare moment, his valet's confused gaze flicked up to his own.

"Nor I, but she has found reason to be unimpressed with the marquis who has been absent so many years, and she has not yet discovered that I am he."

His loyal servant shook his head.

"It's a conundrum," Henry said.

"To be sure. Forgive me. But could you perhaps tell her?"

"I must. I'm seeking a good moment."

The pressed lips of his servant and the silence that followed left Henry guessing any number of things as to the good man's thoughts, but neither said more.

When Henry was at last presentable for more polite society, he stretched and strained against the new cut of his coat.

"My lord?" His valet stepped closer, readjusting the fit and brushing down the shoulders and arms.

"Yes. You are correct. I must tell her." He resisted one final, uncomfortable rotation of his shoulders.

Then he made his way to the carriage.

Today, he had decided to call upon neighbors. He must let it be known that he had returned. Perhaps if the local families began discussing him in favorable ways, he would be seen in a better light by Miss Goodson.

He second-guessed his plan all the way to the Fenningway household, even to the front door. Did he really wish to be known and to have the world understand that he had returned?

For Miss Goodson, he did.

He hoped his plan would work. If he could establish himself back in the neighborhood, if he could win back the hearts of all of his neighbors and friends, perhaps he could also impress the lovely Miss Goodson. When had his every wish become centered around impressing her? She crept in upon him slowly, and he did never expect to be so enamored with the woman, and yet here he was. She was certainly the most interesting of all his associations, as well as the most lovely. And something about her mind, the way that she thought, intrigued him in every way.

The butler opened the door, as stoic as every butler was, standing at about his eye level, and asked, "Whom shall I say is calling?"

"A Lord Wilmington, if you please."

The butler's brow rose, just enough that Henry knew his visit was unexpected and would cause a stir. Again, he wished to escape. But these things could not be avoided. His return to society had been delayed only by the idea that he and Miss

Goodson could interact separately from all of the typical societal norms. But he realized that his selfish desires to keep her to himself were backfiring in every way. And of course, he would need to pay a call to her grandmother. But that call would surely give him away. If only Miss Goodson could stop complaining about the marquis in his presence. His courage failed him every time she did. And what was the worst that could happen? His lips tucked up in the corner, full of chagrin, when he realized she could disdain both Mr. Wardlow and the marquis at the same time while still not knowing they were one and the same.

He was led into a small sitting room. A large crash and the sound of feet running down the stairs surprised him, but he maintained a blank expression. The room was empty.

"Please do be seated." The butler indicated the nearest chair. "The misses will be here to see you shortly."

A sedate and slightly flush-faced woman entered soon after. With a deep, matronly curtsey, she said, "Lord Wilmington. We are honored you would condescend to pay a call."

Henry rose from his bow. "I am returning the favor. It is my understanding that you and your lovely daughters have twice paid a visit to the Wilmington estate."

"We most certainly did. And we enjoyed our tours from your lovely housekeeper. It is a lovely estate. The grounds are lovely. The pond is lovely. You have the finest trees. We could not have been more pleased with everything we saw." The woman's very air breathed elegance.

Henry thought her overly exuberant, certainly, but was pleased with her congenial nature. Perhaps this visit would not be so tedious after all.

Giggling sounded down the hallway, followed by a loud shriek and then more hurried feet. Two young ladies entered in a stately manner, with flushed cheeks. As he studied them, he saw no evidence of the previous ruckus. But he suspected something was amiss.

They were both young, perhaps the same age as Miss Goodson. They were attractive. But nothing like Miss Goodson. He bowed to them both and Mrs. Fenningway said, "These are my daughters, Miss Fenningway and Miss Eliza. I'm pleased to introduce you to Lord Wilmington."

Their curtseys were low and elegant, their hair piled on top of their heads, their cheeks rosy, their lips pursed. In fact, he found it very difficult to tell them apart. Mrs. Fenningway held out her hand. "Please be seated. You do us a great honor by visiting."

"I wish to be involved in the neighborhood. I wish to get to know all our neighbors, and plan to begin hosting in my home," he said.

Mrs. Fenningway sat up taller in her chair, if that were possible, with her stiff posture governing her comfort by the looks of it. And she seemed to barely contain the words that next flowed out. "Oh, ladies, this is excellent news, and we would be more than happy to assist in whatever hosting needs you have. Both of my daughters are accomplished and capable in every way to help in these matters."

He thought her offer overly presumptuous and he was at a loss as to how he would respond. Tea was brought and Mrs. Fenningway gestured for one of her daughters to pour. She took a careful sip. "We have heard most families will return for the holidays."

"For that, I am pleased," Henry said. "Christmas is always better, Twelfth Night as well, when there are more gathered to celebrate."

"And we are dreadfully sorry, and express our deep condolences in the loss of your mother."

"And I thank you. How hard to spend all of one's mourning far from home."

"All the more reason to celebrate now, I would think." Mrs. Fenningway replaced her cup on the saucer and dabbed her lips with a handkerchief. "I wonder if you've heard a most interesting tidbit about the Knickerson sisters?"

"I don't believe I have. I find I'm sadly uninformed."

Mrs. Fenningway went on and on about every person in the neighborhood, or at least it appeared that way. Her daughters didn't say much of anything, but he suspected they had much to say. When Mrs. Fenningway took a breath, he turned to the woman at his left. "Tell me, how do you like to spend your time?"

Mrs. Fenningway interrupted. "Oh, Miss Eliza is by far the most accomplished debutante you will come across. She spends most of her day actively learning and preparing. Her skills on the pianoforte are unmatched in all of Cheshire."

The slight intake of breath and momentary wrinkling of the forehead told Henry that the other sister was none too pleased to hear her mother's remarks. So he turned to her. "And what do you like to do with your spare time?"

"I ..." She glanced at her mother. "Most of all, I prefer riding my horse."

"Do you know, that's excellent news. Perhaps we should all go riding one afternoon."

Miss Eliza at last found her voice. "I should much enjoy that, as I, too, like to be on my horse. You will hardly find a moment when I am not out riding."

Henry wondered how she rode and studied and played the pianoforte with every hour of her day. But he kept his opinions to himself.

"Tell him, Eliza, of your latest poems."

Eliza opened her mouth, but Mrs. Fenningway continued. "She has composed one recently that no one could resist. And it is highly romantic." She fanned herself.

Eliza's cheeks colored.

Perhaps she had normal sensibilities, or at least she would if her mother didn't speak on her behalf.

A footman entered. "A Miss Goodson to see you." He bowed.

The women rose silently. Henry leapt to his feet. This was good news indeed. But how would he avoid what must come to be?

She stepped into the room, her cheeks flushed. Perhaps she had walked all the way? Her gaze immediately fell upon him, and then she stopped. But she recovered well, smiling to all in the room. "I do apologize for my intrusion. But there is a bit of a mishap, you see."

"What has happened? I would be only too happy to assist," Henry said.

Mrs. Fenningway had yet to say anything, but she stepped forward. "Oh, certainly. We shall send the servants posthaste. What has occurred?"

"It's a simple thing, really." Miss Goodson colored again. "I feel perhaps silly even requesting the assistance."

"Would it be easier to show us?" Henry took her hand and placed it on his arm. She smiled gratefully into his face.

"Certainly, that will not be necessary." Mrs. Fenningway stepped closer. "Come, child. How might we be of assistance?" Her large frame wrapped itself around Miss Goodson in what might appear to be a matronly embrace.

Henry was quite cut off from any close contact.

He hoped that Miss Goodson was able to breathe.

But she was soon freed. "I am fine. Really. Just a bit out of breath from my hurrying to your front door. You are kind to receive me. It is but the plight of a child and a silly cat who has found himself quite caught in brambles. The child is beside herself, you see." Miss Goodson shrugged.

Mrs. Fenningway toshed and tsked and was about to throw the whole suggestion away, so Henry said, "Oh dear. Are they your tenants, Mrs. Fenningway?"

She opened her mouth, closed it, and then nodded. "I

presume, if they are within walking distance." She eyed Henry and Miss Goodson and the waiting servant. "Please, allow Miss Goodson to lead you to the child." She lifted a hand. "And send a basket for her family."

"Yes, miss." The footman bowed.

And all waited for Miss Goodson to lead the servant out the door.

"My thanks again." She curtseyed to Mrs. Fenningway, looked once more in Henry's direction, and then left.

"Of all the odd requests." Mrs. Fenningway shook her head. "Well, that's that. Shall we now hear Eliza play?"

Henry was of a mind to go after Miss Goodson, but felt trapped by his hostess. He'd come to call. A part of him was relieved he'd avoided the moment of truth when Miss Goodson would at last realize he was the dreaded marquis—and worse, he hadn't let on about it to her.

When he finally freed himself from the Fenningway home, he knew one thing. He had to tell her himself.

CHAPTER 9

$\mathcal{O}$dette still had not recovered from seeing Mr. Wardlow at the Fenningway home. Paying a call? He'd not paid a call to her grandmother yet. He'd not been by in days, actually, in any way.

She stabbed her needlepoint.

"Careful, dear." Grandmother's eyes were filled with amusement. "Something not sitting right this morning?"

Perhaps she could lay the whole of it out for her grandmother. But she already knew what she would say. Grandmother would not be pleased.

"Tell me again why you are so set on the marquis? I heard today that he neglected to give gifts to any of the servants last year," Odette said.

"If he did, we must blame his steward, though I hardly believe it. That man would not neglect such an important detail."

She pressed her lips together. Somehow, all irritation with Mr. Wardlow, with the Fenningways, with the blasted cat who was stuck in brambles, was being directed solely at the marquis.

Grandmother adjusted her spectacles. "He really is a good man."

"But how can you know? I've seen no evidence to prove your overly high opinion of him."

"You've not met him. How could you have any evidence either way? Be careful your mind is not influenced simply by what you hear. No one in Cheshire knows him overly well at this point."

"Precisely my frustration with the man. He has a duty here. Or he could."

"And do we know that he was not doing his duty here by being away? He has been successful."

Odette huffed.

"What is this about? You seem overly angry towards an innocent man." Grandmother's twinkling amusement did little to assuage Odette's . . . what was it? Her jealousy. She was jealous and betrayed that Mr. Wardlow would pay a social visit to the Fenningways, and not to her. Most especially because her grandmother would perhaps learn to support him as a prospect were she to meet him. She would know what family he was from—apparently he knew the Goodsons. For not the first time, Odette remained frustrated with her lack of time spent in Cheshire. She had arrived at the age of ten, and very soon after was sent to finishing school. Spending only holidays in Cheshire did little to help her know the families in the area.

A small voice asked how she was any different from the marquis himself, as she had spent little time here as well.

She brushed the nagging voice aside. She was home much more than he.

Or so she presumed.

But why had he not come to call?

She stood up. No matter. She was going to put together her Boxing Day event. And it would be more diverting and more important than socializing or pining, or whatever it was she was doing.

"Come, Odette. Tell me what's bothering you."

"I think I shall work with the servants on our Boxing Day plans."

"If you wish, dear."

A footman bowed at the entrance to the room, holding the mail tray.

"Oh, thank you, Thomas, please bring it here," Grandmother said. She sniffed as she took the correspondence. "From the Knickersons."

"Oh?" Odette leaned over her shoulder.

"They wish for us to know that they have been invited to the marquis's home, as special guests, for dinner."

Odette's heart hammered inside.

Grandmother sifted through the other letters. "Perhaps ours has been delayed."

"Perhaps. Or it is because he cannot invite all of the neighborhood at the same time. And if he wants his numbers even, he has three women already in the Knickerson house."

Grandmother patted her hand. "Yes, you are correct, of course." But the worry across Grandmother's brow concerned Odette.

"We shall be perfectly happy here in our own home come Thursday evening."

"Of course we shall." Grandmother's smile was wan.

And Odette felt a sense of excited dread. Was that even possible? She considered her feelings. Certainly, a new hope had fizzled up inside at the mention of the marquis, here in town and throwing a dinner party. But also dread in that she fully expected not to like him, and if that were the case, would Grandmother insist that she attempt to spend time with him? Would he find her equally tiresome?

Grandmother huffed. "I will not have those three lording it over me, pretending that they are more dear to the marquis."

"Grandmother?"

"Well, I won't. They were trouble enough during my Season. I'll not have them be trouble during yours."

"What . . ."

"Never you mind." She reached for a piece of paper. "We shall see what we can figure out, shall we?"

Odette left her grandmother to her business, whatever it might be. She knew it directly affected her in one way or another, but she couldn't bring herself to care as much as Grandmother certainly did. Odette didn't care one whit if she were never invited to the marquis's home. She rather hoped she'd avoid him completely, thus being able to avoid pretending niceties to a man she was sure to dislike. At least that was what she told herself.

But Mr. Wardlow . . . Her heart clenched. She did care about him. And couldn't understand why he stayed away. But there was not much she could do about him. One could not force a gentleman to have interest.

She took the carriage into town. It was time to see if she could drum up some support for Boxing Day. Her first stop would be the Hugheses. Their silk-weaving shop was the finest around. She always felt so much pride in them as tenants on her family's land, as well as successful shop owners.

As she approached, they were outside the front of the shop throwing the silk. She'd seen the process only once before, from afar. She picked up her feet. Mr. Hughes stood on one end of a triangle of people. He held a large, bobbinlike object. From it, strands of silk stretched far, all the way to Mrs. Hughes, who stood a good thirty yards away. A young child took the first rod, containing what looked like four bobbins of silk, and ran it all the way to the end, where Mrs. Hughes stood. They attached it and then he ran back, doing the same with the next bobbins. When she was close enough, Mr. Hughes called out to her. "Good to see you, Miss Goodson."

"And you! Might I watch a moment?"

"Certainly. Our Gerund here will be running for many hours yet."

She expected some kind of groan, but the lad ran by with a cheeky smile, and she laughed. "Well, that is impressive."

"We should calculate sometime just how far I'm running."

"I'd be happy to be of service." Mr. Wardlow's deep voice sent Odette a wash of tingling sensations. Goodness, whatever was this? But she was not going to complain. She turned with a bright smile. "Mr. Wardlow."

He sauntered closer, as though he hadn't a care in the world. "And I cannot even tell you how pleased I am to see you. Hello, Miss Goodson."

Gerund ran by again.

"Oh yes. I have just volunteered for a task, haven't I?" Mr. Wardlow stepped closer. "Tell me, Mr. Hughes, how far are you from the other end?"

"Oh, that's a good thirty yards, give or take."

"Is he stretching it out?"

"A bit, and twisting it, you see." He indicated the rod at his end that was turning.

The lad brought back another set of bobbins.

"And this is so that you can weave?"

"Yes. The missus has some new fabrics all ready if you're wanting to take a look."

"Oh, I am, certainly. Yours are the finest," Mr. Wardlow said.

"We thank you for that. What with these new mills popping up all around, we aren't too certain how long we'll stay in business."

Mr. Wardlow paused in his apparent calculations. "I, too, am very interested. And might I ask, how many rolls will you make today?"

"If we don't tire out, twelve."

Mr. Wardlow's eyes widened, and then he nodded, back to his concentrations.

69

"I'm here hoping to talk to your family about a proposed Boxing Day festivity," Odette said.

"That sounds lovely. You know we are always willing to have a party of some sort," Mr. Hughes said.

"I had hoped you would be interested. I'd like to have it in town, perhaps around the fountain. And invite servants and tenants alike to come, bring gifts for each other in some way? Perhaps we could all bring food to share."

"Well, now that is a beautiful thing to do. I think the town would appreciate the gesture, and it might be the start of a beautiful tradition."

"I'm afraid it is selfishly motivated. I would love to be surrounded by people this Christmas. Our family is down to two, and I must borrow some of yours." She smiled, shaking away the vulnerability of her conversation.

"Well then, we would be proud to be a part." He waved to Mrs. Hughes. "She's finished with her part. Would you like to talk over the details inside?"

"Thank you. I would."

Mr. Wardlow stood taller. "If you finish the twelve rolls today, your son will have run nearly fourteen miles."

"What?!" Odette looked from one to the other.

Gerund just winked as he took another lap.

"That's impressive."

"Would you look at that?" Mr. Hughes ran a hand along his forehead. "I had no idea."

They left him to his wide-eyed thoughts and followed Mrs. Hughes into the shop.

She seemed equally excited about Odette's idea for a Boxing Day celebration and agreed to help spread the word and see who else might want to assist in the planning. "And now I wish to show you our latest designs." She led them to the side of the store with bolts and bolts of fabrics and pulled out one in deep blue. "This would match your complexion perfectly." She held it up to Odette's face and then turned to Mr. Wardlow.

"I agree. You are quite fetching in that color."

"Thank you." She wasn't certain what to do with the attention. But she put several yards on hold, and Mr. Wardlow asked many questions of Mrs. Hughes, questions she was most interested to hear. Shipping details. Trade. Wider sales options for the Hughes family. Was he involved in trade himself?

Would she ever understand this man and where he came from and what he did? She would. She was determined.

But then three giggling women entered the store.

The Fenningways.

Odette instinctually stepped closer to Mr. Wardlow. He tucked her hand on his arm, and seemed to brace for their entrance. How curious. She felt the same way. She put a hand up to her mouth and tried to hide a laugh, but he must have noticed. "Steady."

She snorted. Were they both thinking the same thing?

The ladies turned, and everyone in the near vicinity surely knew the moment they saw Mr. Wardlow.

"Oh my, hello. Goodness, how fortuitous to see you here. We were just looking for the perfect fabric. A ball in Cheshire, for Christmas. We are all aflutter with happiness." Miss Eliza curtseyed low.

Miss Fenningway draped herself all over Mr. Wardlow's other arm, and Miss Eliza joined her. "Are you walking through town? We would love an escort. Mother will linger here, surely, and we were hoping more for the tarts at Grindley's and the tea at Miss Mae's." Miss Fenningway's pout seemed to grow as her eyelashes fluttered.

Mr. Wardlow smiled. "Then we must all make our way there at once." He pressed Odette's hand against his side with the inside of his arm, but she was not participating in this outing. She had no desire to compete with the likes of the Fenningways.

And seeing them fawn all over Mr. Wardlow was making her rather ill.

She dislodged her hand. "Oh, you go ahead. I wasn't quite finished here."

Mr. Wardlow's mouth dropped open and he started to shake his head, which was all rather gratifying.

Miss Eliza stepped in to take his other arm, almost pushing Odette aside, but not quite. With two women talking at once, Mr. Wardlow was led from the store. His last glance over the shoulder at her looked as though the man wished to be rescued, but Odette didn't feel the least sorry for him. If he was going to entertain them, then he was stuck with the results of his actions. If he really wanted to stay with Odette, he would have, or would have insisted she come, or any number of things. All considered, perhaps she'd best become accustomed to the idea that he wasn't pursuing her, or not with any great strength.

CHAPTER 10

*H*enry could not believe Miss Goodson had left him in the clutches of the Fenningways. Why hadn't she wanted to come closer into town with them?

Their chatter was loud and incessant. He had stopped being able to follow either one; they insisted on talking over and around one another, and neither were on the same topic. He used the time instead to ponder over something Odette had said.

She longed to have people around here at Christmastime. Perhaps his ball would do the trick. And at the ball, he would tell her who he was, and she would be so overtaken with the beauty of the season and his gesture that she wouldn't even be angry with him that he'd not disclosed his true identity all this time.

He shook his head.

"Oh, do you not agree? Well, we could certainly wear green. That is also an excellent color for Christmas. I had just thought that red, well, it's such a bright color—leads one to amorous thoughts, don't you think so?" Miss Eliza fluttered her eyelashes and leaned in closer to him.

"Pardon me?" He tried to somehow create distance between him and either lady, but they had hedged him in good.

They found a nice table in the tearoom and were waiting on their tea when he began formulating more of a plan. He'd invited the Knickersons to dinner. He'd learned from Odette that they were always in need of the finer food items, and he had plenty to spare. They would also be excellent practice for when he wished to entertain. Perhaps if he had several of these dinner parties in a row, he could then get himself back out in the society of the neighborhood, spread good feelings about himself, change the gossip to be in his favor, and impress Odette. Then at the ball, he'd be practiced, and his staff prepared, to host so many more at once.

"Oh, Lord Wilmington. I can't tell you how nice it is to have a member of the peerage back in our town." Miss Fenningway looked sensible for a moment, as though the comment were not merely to attempt to flatter and gratify him.

"How so?"

"You are able to influence so many, and your voice is respected. You can host and protect and aid in the social gatherings and in the families that are interested in staying here in Cheshire. Surely, if you deem it worthy, others will as well."

An itch of guilt nagged at him, for he'd been considering leaving as soon as Twelfth Night finished. Until he'd met Miss Goodson. But if she was not interested in pursuing more with him, he might leave before. He'd try his dinner parties and ball and see where that got him as far as she was concerned. Otherwise, he was more than happy to let a place in London and take care of his shipping business.

"I see. Well, I am honored to be here at our family's estate. I have large and noble shoes to fill, certainly. But I shall attempt to do my best. Will either of you have a Season in London?"

"Oh, we most certainly will. If you are attending the Season, we shall be so much more comfortable. We've never been to London. Mother says we will be great successes there because of our deportment." Miss Fenningway shrugged. "But who can say.

The women seem so elegant in all the pictures we see in the paper."

"I cannot say, myself, I've been away so long. But the two of you are as elegant as any."

Both turned the deepest shade of pink, and he realized that perhaps he should keep his compliments to a minimum. Or perhaps he shouldn't compliment at all.

"Oh, you are too kind. Thank you!" Miss Eliza dipped her head. "We do worry so."

"At any rate, we are pleased you have returned." Miss Fenningway leaned towards him, as if waiting for him to say more. But he had no desire to expound upon his leaving and why he'd stayed away so long. During that period, it had seemed the most important use of his time. Every week, he knew if he stayed on another week, they would be that much more successful. It seemed worth it then.

Until life at home passed him by.

He held back the sigh that might have lessened the tightness that always built up in his chest. There was still much to salvage here. He would, of course, be more aware of his duties in Cheshire, but besides Odette, he saw no reason why he could not spend all of his time in Town, and closer to his ships.

He had no idea what they were chattering about, but somewhere in the middle of their conversations, he interrupted with, "Would you like to join me for a dinner party at my home?"

They were silent for a moment, and then the chattering began again.

Miss Eliza's grin filled her face. "Oh, I'd love to. If you are in need of any assistance in the planning or hostessing, I would be more than happy—"

"I, as well, am well trained in any of those areas," Miss Fenningway said. "I am pleased to assist in making suggestions for whom to invite, as you will need to balance out the numbers, certainly. And we have lived here our whole lives."

"I would appreciate that very much, thank you."

"I shall come up with a list this very afternoon and ask a servant to deliver it," Miss Fenningway said.

"Or I could come deliver it myself," Miss Eliza added.

"Yes, we could come and assist in the planning this very afternoon if you like."

"Thank you so much for all your assistance. I would appreciate the expertise, and I'm certain my servants would love to go over the details with you."

They seemed to deflate somewhat at the mention of servants. "And I, myself, of course would love to hear your thoughts."

They perked back up considerably at that comment.

One thing this outing was showing him was that finding a wife to help in these areas would not be too difficult. But finding one he cared to be with, that would be more so. Especially if she did not care to be with him.

Again, he puzzled over why Odette had not agreed to come.

At last, the outing came to an end. When he stopped back by the Hughes' spinning shop, Gerund was still out there running and twisting the silk. He waved to the cheery lad and his pa and made his way back into the shop. He'd seen Miss Goodson eyeing a particular silk, and he wanted to see what it could be made into.

LATER THAT EVENING, his servants were setting the grand table in anticipation of the Knickerson sisters. He had asked that they use all the finery, and he'd invited two widowers and a couple who lived on the other side of his estate. But he'd omitted the Goodsons, and he knew that would be seen as a sharp oversight by Mrs. Goodson if she were to hear of it. But he selfishly couldn't bring himself to invite Odette yet. It would be the admitting of his deception. And he wasn't on great footing with her right now.

Did he have a deception? Not really. He'd merely allowed

her to believe something that wasn't true. She'd arrived at her errant conclusions all on her own.

He knew it was still a deception.

But he couldn't face things quite yet. First, he must be on better relations with her.

When the servants announced each guest, they expressed such happiness at once again being in the home, at the fact that he was entertaining. That the neighborhood needed him. He felt gratified. Immediately, he began planning his next dinner.

And other good things were being realized. He could have been mistaken, but Miss Knickerson, who had never been married, seemed quite taken with the widower Mr. Thompson. Perhaps Henry was a matchmaker on top of it all.

The dinner went on, and he saw how much he should have included Mrs. Goodson. When Miss Knickerson mentioned her, almost in pity, as uninvited, he knew he had made a mistake indeed. With the obvious exclusion of his closest neighbor, he'd made some sort of statement. When the men finished their port and rejoined the ladies, he excused himself for a moment. In his study, he pulled out a parchment and began drafting a letter.

A short stack of correspondence sat at his right elbow. And at the top of the stack was a letter with the Goodson seal on it.

Chagrined, he opened it.

Dear Lord Wilmington,

Well I remember all your afternoons spent with dear Mr. Goodson, may he rest in peace. I have missed you both dearly. Him because he was the companion of my heart, and you because you brought such a youth and happiness to his face. I have heard you are returned. I wanted to express my great happiness to hear of such a thing, and to invite you to come pay a call on an old friend at your earliest convenience.

We await your visit.

Sincerely,
Mrs. Goodson

SHE SIGNED IT SIMPLY, as though they were family or friends. And he felt warmed toward the woman, and terrible in derelict of duty. How could he have neglected his duty to such a sorry state?

Miss Goodson or no, he owed an apology to her grandmother.

And in deference of her husband, the late Mr. Goodson, he left his own dinner party as they wrapped up their whist games, and with a satchel full of dinner items, wrapped carefully by his cook, he walked down the lane toward the Goodson home.

CHAPTER 11

*O*dette wore her most comfortable house dress. She and
Grandmother sat together in the library with a large fire
blazing, filling the smaller room with heat. A grand blanket
draped over the both of them, Odette read aloud from their latest
story.

Then the door opened and the servant announced, "The
Marquis of Wilmington to see you."

Odette and her grandmother both gasped at once.

"At this hour?" Odette raised a hand to her hair, knowing that
tendrils had fallen loose from her low bun and were all about her
face. She turned an accusatory glare at her grandmother.

"I cannot explain it."

"Are you certain? Because last I left you, something was
afoot with that gleam in your eye."

Grandmother laughed. "I did write him a letter. It was an
invitation to come at his earliest convenience. Goodness. I guess
that is right now."

They looked at each other and then Grandmother shrugged.
"We may as well receive him in here as anywhere."

"Like this?"

"I suppose so." She laughed. "Let him know how we really are straight off the bat, correct?"

"I like the way you think." Odette lifted the blanket off their lap. "Perhaps we shall look like we are not already abed on the couch, though." She laughed.

She knew this meeting was important to her grandmother, and so a part of her softened. She might not have high expectations for the man, but she absolutely knew that her grandmother was pleased to have him stop by. Although the hour was completely odd.

"Isn't he hosting a dinner party this very evening?" Odette had seen four carriages pull up to his home. Though Grandmother hadn't mentioned the Knickersons' invitation again, Odette knew it had hurt her feelings to be excluded from such a group.

Grandmother stood and straightened out her skirts. "Perhaps you should go attend to yourself, if but a small amount. First impressions, you know." Her eyes were kind, and so full of hope, Odette couldn't refuse the woman.

"Very good. I shall return shortly." She kissed Grandmother on the cheek and then made her way upstairs.

What should she wear? Something obviously meant to impress? Something effortless? She wasn't certain how to go about this at all.

When at last she returned, she found a smiling Grandmother with a tray full of food, and no marquis.

"Has he gone?"

"He said he is in the middle of entertaining, and he realized his great error in not inviting me to his first dinner upon returning, so he personally brought some of the dinner over to share." She laughed. "He is as much a dear of a man as I remember him being as a boy. He really is special, Odette. And so caring. He's missing Mr. Goodson." Her dear grandmother's face crinkled in happy tears. "I cannot help myself. It's the holidays, you know. And he did so love to fish with your grandfather."

Odette handed over a handkerchief, at once intrigued by such a man. The kindness, the gentleness, that his visit had created such a response in her grandmother. She was touched indeed, and considered that perhaps she would need to rethink her opinions of him.

She sat across from her grandmother at the desk in the library, and they tasted bits of the marquis's gifted dinner.

"His cook is quite excellent." Grandmother placed another piece of the mutton in her mouth. "The meat is so soft and savory. I know it is late, but this tastes wonderful."

A man stepped back into the room.

"Oh!" Odette jumped.

Mr. Wardlow waved his hands. "Please, stay seated. Hello, Miss Goodson." He bowed. "I came from dinner just now."

"You were also invited?" She shook her head, astounded at how many of their acquaintances had been included on this first dinner list.

"Oh, well . . ."

Grandmother eyed her with significant confusion.

She didn't know quite what to say. And how had Mr. Wardlow just walked into their home unannounced? Where were the servants?

"Grandmother. This is the man I've long been wanting to introduce you to, Mr. Wardlow. And this is Mrs. Goodson, my grandmother."

"Oh yes, we have long been acquainted as well. The Wardlow family dearly loves the Goodsons." His eyes held a certain intensity as he said these last words to her grandmother, who looked from one to the other in a grand confusion. Was she perhaps starting to show the signs of age?

"Grandmother?" Odette placed a hand on her forearm.

"Oh, forgive me. Woolgathering. It has been an age, hasn't it?"

He bowed with what looked like a flash of relief across his face.

"Would you like to join us for dinner? We were pleased to receive such delicate samples from the marquis's estate."

"Uh, certainly. I'd love to join you." He stretched his neck a moment against his cravat and then sat at Odette's side.

"So, tell me, how have you two met?" Grandmother watched them both very closely.

Mr. Wardlow could be nothing but charming and gentleman-like, though arriving at this hour would hardly be smiled upon. Except for the fact that Grandmother's beloved marquis had done just that moments before.

"We met on the lane, actually. She was standing at the side of the path, in what I thought a desperate position, looking for a ride on my equipage."

"I was, in fact, simply out for a walk. But his horses, they prance. They're delightful. So I couldn't resist a swift ride down a few of our lanes before I was rescued and returned home." Odette laughed.

"And we seemed to have the uncanny ability to bump into one another as it were. Today, at the silk weavers' . . ."

"Not that row of mills." Grandmother put a hand at her heart.

"No, certainly not. But the dear Hugheses," Odette said.

"Oh, yes, I love their work. Some of our draperies were made by them."

"Which reminds me, I set aside some bolts of blue silk, if we could perhaps use them for something. It was a lovely shade of blue."

Odette smiled from one to the other. At last, Mr. Wardlow might be seen as a potential possibility for her. "Would you both mind sharing some stories of Cheshire? I was not able to grow up here. And I would love to learn more about how you met."

"We first saw . . . Mr. Wardlow . . . when he was a babe. His mother was recovering well, and we brought over a gift to celebrate. We were ushered right in and given a peek at the beautiful son they'd just birthed." Grandmother smiled, a small, tender look. "Well I remember that day. Your parents were dear friends, the best kinds."

"I know they always felt the same for you." He rested a hand over top her grandmother's, and for a moment, she couldn't remember why on earth there had ever been a concern about Mr. Wardlow in her grandmother's eyes.

"Your name. Wardlow. I'd forgotten."

His eyes sharpened for a moment and flitted up into her grandmother's face. "Many people do."

"What? They forget your name?"

"Certainly. I suppose it is unremarkable."

Odette shook her head in confusion. "I don't really see how that would be the case."

"Tell me of the orchards. Do they still bear fruit?" Mr. Wardlow asked.

"Orchards?" Odette said.

"Yes, he's speaking of the brambly section of our estate, almost taken over by the wilds. I believe there is fruit to be had in that corner. For the brave."

He sat up taller. "I believe we are the brave. I remember your apples are the finest in England. Would you mind terribly if I carved a path into the brambles?"

"I wouldn't mind a bit. If you bring me an apple, I shall be all the more grateful."

"Might I ask for the company of Miss Goodson? Perhaps she can pick the best path?"

Grandmother opened her mouth and then closed it again.

Odette held her breath. Knowing Grandmother much preferred the marquis, she could only guess at the inner struggle, but when at last she nodded, Odette could only breathe out in relief.

"Oh thank you, Grandmother. If only I'd known sooner. We might be eating apple pie in the evenings."

Grandmother smiled. "Please take servants with you. And then certainly. Our estate has always been yours."

"And mine yours. I appreciate very much all these years of living near . . ." Mr. Wardlow stopped, and he glanced at Odette.

"So, did you just run home from here when you were a lad?" She considered all the close estates. All were accounted for in her mind.

"He always came and went as he pleased around here. His parents tried their best with him." Grandmother laughed.

He shook his head.

"Tell Odette about your times in the mud."

"Oh, I'm sure she doesn't wish to hear."

"Believe me. She would."

He laughed. "There were a few times that I was undeniably more of a ruffian than any sort of gentleman."

"That, I can well believe. Did you know, Grandmother, that I saw him up on the roof of the Knickersons' home?"

"She saw me falling off, to be precise."

Grandmother laughed again. "I do believe you." She waved her hand for Mr. Wardlow to continue.

"The local families became very accustomed to seeing me run here and there. Even in the rain. So one day, I was out running about, and I fell, and had a bit of a scrape on my knee. Being a young lad, and not as tough as I am now, I cried long rivers through the mud on my cheeks and found my way to the front door here."

Odette smiled, trying to imagine a young and crying Mr. Wardlow.

"I was covered in mud, quite literally, but somehow your butler recognized me and allowed me in. They shuffled me down

84

to the cook, who cleaned me off—with warm water, even—and sent me off with a tin of biscuits, no less."

"How lovely." Odette could only be proud of their excellent staff.

"Yes, until one considers the tracks."

"Tracks?"

"Yes, the muddy remains I left on every surface I touched."

Odette smiled. "And there were many, no doubt. Surfaces."

"Certainly. Every place I went. Father found out somehow about the servants' great kindness, and he sent over a gift basket for them all . . . and . . ."

"And?"

"And myself to come clean up the mud."

"No!" Odette laughed.

"Yes. Of course, the servants had already cleaned up all the mud. So I was simply given some cake in the kitchen, treated royally, and then sent on my way, much more contrite about the work I caused others."

"Why, that's an excellent lesson, then."

"It was. Their kindness taught me more than any punishment ever could."

"Grandmother, did you know all this was going on?"

"I certainly did. And was pleased as punch. This lad here has always had a place in our home, if he wanted it."

Mr. Wardlow smiled so warmly at her grandmother that Odette became all the more confused.

But then he stood. "I do apologize for my abrupt arrival and departure. But I should return to the party, and I will arrive early tomorrow for our first efforts in accessing the delectable apples."

"Very good. I'll see you then." Odette stood and walked him to the door.

After it was shut, she whirled around. "Grandmother! What did you think?"

But Grandmother had a deep frown on her face.

"What is it?"

"Oh, it is nothing, child."

"But why are you frowning?"

"I am puzzling. That is very different from frowning."

"It looks much like a frown on my end."

"Well, I don't know if I'm necessarily having a negative thought, though it appears quite negative on the outside. I'm puzzling, child. That's the best I can do."

"But do you like Mr. Wardlow?"

"I . . . do."

"You approved our walk to the old orchards tomorrow."

"I did."

"Then might I see him if I so wish?"

"You . . . you might."

But she could not make here nor there of her grandmother's very cryptic and noncommittal responses. "Thank you."

"Shall we be off to our beds now? This cozy, easy evening has turned out to be very busy indeed."

"I'm sorry to have missed the marquis. Was he everything you remembered?"

Grandmother ran a hand over her face. "And more." Then she smiled. "But things are going very well, all things considered. It was wonderful to see our dear marquis once again, and to meet your Mr. Wardlow."

Odette nodded, and with a slight skip to her step, kissed Grandmother on the cheek. "Good night, my dearest grandmother."

"Good night, my dearest Odette."

CHAPTER 12

*H*enry had made a complete blunder there. He kicked at a bit of something on his walk back to his home. How had he been in the Goodson home with Mrs. Goodson and Odette and still been confused for Mr. Wardlow? Why did Mrs. Goodson play along? He threw his hands up in the air. And why hadn't he simply confessed?

A coward. He'd turned into a coward. One look in Odette's eyes, and he quaked before the fear of her displeasure.

Well, he couldn't continue forever, and if he didn't come clean soon, he might *lose* her forever. And how would that feel?

With these thoughts plaguing him the whole of the night, he returned the very next morning to pay a call at the Goodson home.

The butler announced him into the front sitting room. "A Lord Wilmington to see you."

But Mrs. Goodson sat alone.

Henry clenched his hat in his hands, feeling strengthened by its presence. He stood tall, and forced his feet into the room.

"Ah, I've been hoping you would return, Lord Wilmington."

She nodded. "Please be seated. Have some tea. You'll forgive me if I don't call Odette down just yet."

"I imagine you have questions."

"And I was hoping you had answers." She smiled and handed him a cup. "I don't recall if I have poured your tea before. Something tells me you are a one sugar sort of person."

He nodded.

"And extra strong."

He nodded again. With a small sip, he grinned, or perhaps it was a grimaced sort of smile. "It is just how I like it." Then he placed the cup on the saucer and leaned forward. "Miss Goodson is under the impression that I am a gentleman farmer, I believe? Someone, at any rate, by the name of Mr. Wardlow."

"At first, we thought you a tenant."

He cleared his throat. "I know I am a bit unconventional, particularly since my return, but I assure you I have always behaved as a gentleman should, at least I hope as much."

Mrs. Goodson's eyebrows rose. "And your solitary rides in the phaeton?"

He shifted. "That was one time, and she was walking alone." His turn to raise eyebrows did not feel as satisfactory. "Though I do understand that was not the thing. I am out of practice, and once she was beside me, I quite enjoyed myself to the point of taking a longer route home, I admit it."

She nodded, but there was a slight twinkle in her eyes that eased his discomfort somewhat.

"I care for her. I'd like to court her." The words came out through a tightness in his throat. "But she greatly dislikes the marquis."

"You talk of him as though you are not the same person."

"I know. And that's the difficulty. Because the way she views him, I don't understand how we could be. To her, he is neglectful, selfish and . . ." He dropped his head, seeking out the tips of his boots. "I suppose I do resemble him."

"Not at all. You're as much the dear boy I knew now as you were then."

Hope warmed him, but fizzled again as he contemplated his dilemma.

"My concern is not who or what the marquis was, but instead, who he has become. It's the deception. Why are we in this situation to begin with?" Mrs. Goodson asked.

Henry slumped his shoulders but met her gaze. "I cannot even recall fully. In my defense, I have spent little time home, and often don't consider myself the marquis while in the East Indies. I know that is weak, but I'm a Wardlow. And then when I heard she so disdains the marquis, how could I own up to the identity when she looks so pleasingly upon Mr. Wardlow?"

"Should I be concerned that you speak of yourself as though you were outside your body?"

He chuckled. "Perhaps I should be concerned at such a thing. But I've come to make amends. Today. I wish to come clean. To tell her the truth and to respectfully ask to court her."

"You mustn't. Not yet."

His mouth dropped open. "Mrs. Goodson, I'm afraid I must."

"Allow her to learn something good of you first, as the marquis. Allow her to ease into the understanding that she has been so wrong about you, for that is half the battle here. Not only will you have to change her mind, but you have to help her see she is wrong."

"Perhaps not anyone's preference."

"Not at all."

"But do you think? Is there any part of her that might be . . . pleased I am the marquis?"

Mrs. Goodson's long pause and then the pursing of her lips did not bring any comfort to Henry, not a bit.

At last, she merely shrugged. "Who's to say? She's not the kind to care overly about a person simply because of a title. What she will love is that you live here, that your property abuts ours, and that she can continue her life in much the way she does while she is here."

His heart sank a bit.

"But I hear you are to let a house in London?"

He should not be surprised that people knew these things, and yet he always was. "I am."

"And have an active shipping business?"

"I do."

"And perhaps wish to travel?"

"Perhaps."

And there, perhaps, lay his greatest trouble. "So, what you are saying is that I not only have to convince her of her error, convince her that the marquis is in fact a good man—I hope I might call myself such—but in addition, I need to consign myself to a life here at my estate?"

"Or convince her that she desires above all to be abroad." Mrs. Goodson clucked. "Come, it will be simpler than you imagine, for she's half in love with you already."

His heart pounded so loudly, he doubted his hearing. "What's that you say?"

"Oh, she is. Mark my words. Her Mr. Wardlow is the sun, moon, and stars at the moment."

He liked the sound of that.

"And the marquis is the cause of all her frustrations," Mrs. Goodson continued.

He shook his head. "What must I do?"

"What you are doing is excellent. Invite the people over. Remind them who you are. Word will spread."

"I do believe inviting the Knickersons might assist in the spreading?"

"Oh yes, most definitely."

"And you know I should have come calling long before now, if just for our long-held and dear relationship." He dipped his head. "I have felt regret at feeling separate from you while trying to hide my identity." He rotated his shoulders. "All this sounds so terribly devious. And I promise I am not so. I don't know what's come over me."

"Perhaps love."

Henry studied Mrs. Goodson's face. She was serious. He knew he should consider love. He was thinking of altering his life for this woman—surely that counted for something close to love, if not exactly love. He would have to see. What knew he of love? He had best learn.

"I do wish to warn you. The more popular you become here in Cheshire, the more she might complain about you."

"Well, that seems a bit against our purposes, does it not?"

"No, that is perfect. It means she is starting to be intrigued, wants to know you against her better judgment, and that is right where you want her."

"So, I should tell her while she is complaining?"

"Absolutely not."

"I don't understand. I am to tell her, aren't I?"

"You are to show her. Invite her to your ball, and show her then."

"I'm not certain . . ."

"And while you're at it, assist her with her Boxing Day plans. This is the most important thing for her right now. She's spent hours."

He nodded, still unsure about waiting until the ball to show her who he really was, but happy to assist with Boxing Day. "I believe I'm already assisting with the actual packaging of the gifts we are giving."

"No, not *you* you. The *marquis*, you. He must assist."

"Excellent. But help without being seen?"

"Precisely."

Henry sighed. This was all much more complicated than he felt it needed to be. But he wanted more than anything to convince Miss Goodson that he was worthy of her time and her love. He swallowed. Things had certainly increased in importance in the few moments he'd spent with Mrs. Goodson. The word love had been mentioned multiple times. He sat up taller. "And now, perhaps, I might go for a walk with Miss Goodson to explore the apple orchards?"

A servant was tasked with fetching her. Henry was full of misgivings about continuing his charade. Had he not spent the night convincing himself that he should bare all to Miss Goodson? He had.

When she stepped into the front room, her face full of bright smiles all directed at him, he questioned his ability to do anything other than continue to make her smile.

"And how are you this fine morning, Mr. Wardlow?"

"I'm well, and by the looks of you, you're simply ravishing this morning, am I correct?"

Her cheeks flamed, but she laughed it off. "I'm well, just as you." She shook her head. "And what are we to do today?"

"Do?"

"Yes, you always come with some grand plan or other."

He faltered a moment and then grinned. "I do, don't I?" He held out his arm. "Today, I'm hoping that you might collect your warmer clothes, and we will go for a walk."

"A walk?"

"Yes. We mentioned the orchards, but there is much to explore and I'm almost certain not an apple to be found in December."

"I love walks."

"As do I. I feel we are most suited in this thing."

"And while we walk, we might perhaps hunt down some greenery?"

"Oh, most excellent. For we are simply bare at the moment. Not a single décor."

"As are we, as you can see, but it is not Christmas Eve. We have a week to prepare, have we not?"

"We most certainly do. And I have decided right now in this moment that you and I must prepare together."

"Oh?" Her smile of pleasure caused an equally large grin on his own face.

"Yes, so I must see your list."

"My list?"

"I know you have one. Of all the things you are doing to prepare for the festivities this season, for Boxing Day, for Christmas Eve, for Twelfth Night. Let's start working on your list."

Miss Goodson looked a bit like she might be overcome with glee. But she bounced a moment and then nodded. "I shall get my warmer things and my list, and return shortly." She gripped her skirts and rushed from him.

"Oh, you have made her happy, indeed." Mrs. Goodson surprised Henry as she wiped a bit of something at the corner of her eye. "I pray you don't break her heart." She turned, and with that foreboding comment, left him alone in the front entryway.

He, too, wanted that least of all. In fact, he'd do anything to prevent such a thing. This game her grandmother suggested and that he had begun was risky indeed. For if he told her now who he really was, he could risk not having her at all. She might be intrigued by him, but he didn't believe she liked Mr. Wardlow enough to stick with him if he was also the loathsome marquis. Which he was. But if he waited until he could perhaps win her heart, and she did not accept him, they would both be broken.

He quaked at the risk, and had half talked himself into baring all to her, but then she returned, and her light chased the darkness of his thoughts away again.

CHAPTER 13

With Odette's fingers tightly gripping Mr. Wardlow's arm, they made their way out into the brisk air. "It has been unseasonably cold," she said.

"I agree. Perhaps another ice-skating afternoon is in order. Surprisingly, we haven't had much snow."

"Yet. One of the Knickersons told me her elbow is aching, and so she fully expects snow this season."

"Noted. I shall have to remember this unique ability she has to predict the weather."

"I as well, especially if she proves correct." Odette tugged his arm. "We should get our cart from the barn."

"Oh yes, good idea. We would perhaps not enjoy as much of the walk, but carrying the greens will be much simpler with the cart."

"And our ponies could use the exercise."

"To the barn, it is."

They walked with almost a skip in their step. She was so pleased at his suggestion of help. "You know, I am most looking forward to Boxing Day."

"And I'm certain your servants will appreciate your efforts."

"And the tenants. I've moved the whole of it to the fountain in the center of town."

"I recall. What a wonderful notion!"

"Thank you. I do believe they shall appreciate the event."

They attached the ponies to the cart, and then Mr. Wardlow took the reins, his strong hands expertly guiding the ponies out into the yard and then down the lane.

"We turn up this path here to find the best pine cones and the greenery that may have fallen."

"Excellent." He breathed in with a smile. "That smell. It's the best in the world. How would you describe it?"

"Oh, that's very tricky. Pine is . . . well, it's a fresh smell, isn't it?"

"It reminds me of snow. But I think that's because I'm here at home mostly over the holidays, and it often snows. It's also a nutty smell? Or one of spice? Though I mostly associate spice with the East Indies."

"Do you know much about the East Indies, then?"

He hesitated. The marquis had come from there, had Mr. Wardlow as well? "I have just come from there, in fact."

"Tell me about it all."

"I was about to mention the spices. They fill the air. People come to sell them at market. They cover the dirt with their blankets in rows and rows, and they sell spices and their other wares."

"That sounds so different from anything I've ever seen."

"They carry huge exotic birds on their shoulders. Monkeys too."

She wished she could see the places he talked of, at least in her mind. "I've never even seen much of England."

"Would you like to see more?"

"I'd love to see the Lake District again. It's not far. Wales. I've not been to Wales, as close as it is. Can you believe it?"

"Yes, you've been gone most of your years." He shrugged. "But tell me, would you like to see things, outside of England?"

"Far away? Like travel to the East Indies?" She pondered his question, and she knew the answer was yes. But she hesitated. Somehow, she suspected that if she were to admit to a secret desire to sail away on a ship, he could grant it. She didn't know how—it didn't make sense that he would—but she suspected he could. And she was afraid. Wishing to do something and actually doing it were two very different things.

"Yes, exactly that. Or anywhere. Do you dream of visiting far-off places?" He watched her closely, but attempted to make light. She could tell by the careful way he watched her that for some reason, this conversation had far greater significance to him.

"Oh, who can say? I'll never do so. Grandmother needs me. Cheshire needs me. I'm not like some of our neighbors, who seem to completely disregard how their presence or absence might affect a place." She looked away, then pointed. "We're coming up on a good batch of greenery."

The trees in this part of the estate were shorter, and the branches were lower to the ground. Pine cones littered the area at their feet, and branches were easy to collect.

Odette held a branch up to her face and breathed in. "Heavenly."

Mr. Wardlow pulled out a knife and used it to snip it from the tree. They went about collecting the fullest, most healthy-looking choices. Soon, they had a sufficient amount of boughs for at least the first bit of decorating. Mr. Wardlow stood at her side. The woods were quiet and their puffs of air visible as they surveyed their collection.

"I do believe we've done well today, what say you?" His grin was contagious.

"I have to agree. And now, perhaps you'd like to come help get these up on the mantel."

"Absolutely. We'll know how much more to collect if we begin, don't you think?"

"Yes, how big . . ." She stopped herself. "That is to say, how much do you think you will need?" She knew so little of his situation here in Cheshire. Was he in one of the smaller estates that filled the outlying land around the city center? There were quite a few, as the land here was fertile and the silk industry growing.

"I fear we shall need another excursion, at least one, in order to do my home justice."

She nodded. "Excellent, then we shall have another excuse for a walk."

"Or a ride in the pony cart, depending."

He turned to her, his eyes sparkling with the light she was so accustomed to seeing there. For a moment, their eyes connected. Nothing more was said. But with the beauty all around them, the intoxicating smells of the pine and the earth and the freshness that promised snow, she was mesmerized. He stepped closer and reached for her hands. "Miss Goodson."

She swallowed. "Yes?" Her voice had a bit of a croak to it. She cleared her throat. His soft features, his strong jawline, the line of freckles at his cheekbones carried her gaze around his face like a carnival. And then she stopped on his lips. They were full, more full than she'd realized before. And soft looking, velvety, like a cushion almost. When people kissed, did they just connect right there? Did her lips feel as soft as his looked? Did they move? Linger? Or did they press and then part? Where she'd given the whole subject of kissing little thought before, now it was of the most immediate fascination and need. She moved closer. A thick and chunky snowflake fell down between them. "What?" she asked.

Flakes started falling all around them—gathered, wonderful clumps of snow. "Goodness, this is coming down fast," she said.

"It's fascinating." Mr. Wardlow held out his hand to capture the flakes on his mittens.

She stepped closer as they studied the tiny white shapes, joining to make such a remarkable softness from the sky. When she looked up again, he was close, nearer than ever before. His gaze moved over her face like a caress. "Thank you," she whispered.

"For what?"

"All this. For . . ." What was she thanking him for? For the wonderful feelings she had whenever they were together? "For decorating with me?" She shrugged.

"You're welcome." His voice was deep, rumbling. It entered her very center and wreaked a sort of brilliant havoc before lingering there and soaking in. She shivered.

"Would you like my cloak?"

"Oh, no, I'm perfectly warm. Thank you." Her cheeks heated. Would he know that his nearness had such a warming effect?

The ground at their feet was dusted with white now, just enough to leave hints of the earth beneath. "It's going to cover everything soon. I guess Miss Knickerson's elbow is right," Odette said.

The corner of his mouth lifted in a tiny grin, but he dipped his head. "I suppose we must make our way back."

"Perhaps the servants can take the cart? And we can walk?"

"In the snow?"

"Oh yes! I'm loathe to leave this magic." She lifted her chin, feeling the soft tickling effect of flakes falling on her face.

"Then we shall walk, certainly." He waved to the servants.

As the pony cart drove out of sight, they were left with only the soft sounds of falling snow. He reached for her hand. "May I?"

She nodded. And even gloved as they were, she enjoyed the thrill of walking hand in hand. For a time, neither said anything. The snow fell all around them in a soft wonder, and Odette enjoyed the quiet. Then Mr. Wardlow began to hum. And somehow the world became more magical. His lively rendition of "God Rest Ye Merry Gentlemen" added some energy to her steps. They both stepped higher and faster to the beat of the music. And then Mr. Wardlow burst forth in song.

Odette laughed, and then she joined him in singing. A bird flew, startled from the branches of a nearby tree. The forest around them filled with song, and Odette laughed while she sang.

God rest ye merry gentlemen let nothing you dismay.
Remember Christ our Savior was born on Christmas Day.
To save us all from Satan's power when we were gone astray.
Oh, tidings of comfort and joy, comfort and joy.
Oh, tidings of comfort and joy.

On they walked and more they sang until most carols had been thoroughly enjoyed. They arrived back at the house with Odette slightly out of breath, cheeks aching from the joy of smiling so much, and generally happier than she'd been in a long time.

Grandmother watched from an upper window. Odette waved. She seemed pleased.

"I think you've won over my grandmother."

"Have I?" Mr. Wardlow lifted his chin to follow Odette's gaze. "Perhaps I have. She's a good woman. Has your best interests at heart."

"She really does. She's not feeling well." The worry she'd been keeping at bay flooded her heart in that moment. "I hope it is a passing thing and she will return to full health come summer, when she can be outside in the air and walking among the flowers."

"I as well. The Goodsons are a wonderful family. They are some of the foundation of Cheshire, they and the Marquis of Wilmington."

Odette snorted before she could stop herself. "Oh, pardon me." She looked away.

"Now, why this disdain? You might enjoy him were you to meet him."

"I might. Everyone else in Cheshire seems to have already seen him or talked with him or been invited to dinner."

"Not quite everyone."

"Even you." She shrugged. "And I cannot account for everyone's sudden acceptance of the man who has neglected us all for so long."

"Perhaps he had his reasons. And has he neglected anyone, really?"

Odette bit her tongue. She would not call out the fact that in her mind, he'd been away when his mother needed him most. That seemed too harsh a judgment to vocalize too often or in this moment, though she had her inner concerns regarding his behavior.

"I don't know, really. Who can say? You are correct in that I should not hold on to feelings for a person I don't know, feelings that are based on very limited knowledge." She huffed out a breath. "I shouldn't, and yet it seems so easy to do so."

"I'm uncertain why that happens, really. But I do know that when someone becomes our friend, or even our acquaintance, it is more difficult to hold them to past grudges. Is it not?"

"You are correct. I'm certain I'll mend my ways when I finally meet the man. Though he's hurt Grandmother dreadfully by neglecting to include her in his invitations. She was unhappy when the Knickersons sent news of their invitation."

He seemed pained by this announcement, as though he had some sort of say in the matter. What a generous man, so intent on caring for others. She smiled at him. "Don't overly concern yourself. It is certainly not *your* doing."

He choked in response, turning away. "Forgive me. It must be the cold air."

They turned at the doorstep. The ground was well and truly covered now. Even their footsteps were filling again with snow.

"But he sent a note. He brought food. Grandmother was a changed woman at the gesture and in that instance, I softened towards him. I thought him…a dear." She shrugged.

Mr. Wardlow nodded, clearing his throat yet again. "I best be going now, but I wonder, with all this snow, might I return in a sleigh?" His eyes were bright with promises.

"Oh, I'd love that, yes, please."

"Excellent. We shall explore the wonders the snow leaves us together, then." He bowed over her hand and then took his leave with a crisp step. She sighed. In her mind, Mr. Wardlow was more wonderful every time they were together, and yet she knew less about him, or so it seemed.

CHAPTER 14

*H*enry arrived home to a stack of invitations. "What's this?"

The butler bowed. "These have all come while you were away."

"Even in all this snow?"

"Perhaps many are anxious to reacquaint themselves with the family?"

He lifted a stack of at least twenty. "Must I attend?"

His butler eyed him for a moment and then dipped his head. "I fear I am not the best person to advise on such issues. I do know that your parents made certain to keep relationships with neighbors they cared for. They also spent time with those they felt they could assist, and because your father was who he was, they did not neglect the tenants or the servants."

Henry nodded. "And so I could perhaps use some counsel so as to understand who is who from this stack?"

"Certainly. Finding a wife, forgive me, would be most advisable. But perhaps Mrs. Taylor could also aid in those matters."

Henry nodded, trying to make sense of his new task. "Excellent. Do we have the attachments for the sleigh?"

"We do indeed, my lord. Shall I ask that they be assembled?"

"Yes, please. I feel we might use them to assist, and also, I have a particular reason for wishing to have them ready."

"Very good." He bowed and left Henry to himself and his correspondence. As he made his way to the study and began opening each one, he began to feel tired. He was to attend each engagement? To support the neighbors? He knew he could discern and would ask the housekeeper, but he assumed at this early stage of his reentry, most would be wise to accept, especially as he wished to make a good name for himself.

And what if Miss Goodson would also be present?

He hung his head in his hands. This was not going to work out in his favor.

Today was an improvement with her, he had to admit. He'd held her hand for that glorious walk in the snow. And she'd agreed to the sleigh ride. But she'd still spoken ill of the marquis . . . and then slightly recanted? Perhaps he'd changed her mind?

Who could know.

He would find out soon enough. He frowned. Why had her grandmother thought it best to keep up the charade? He did not agree with the woman. Perhaps she knew best? Miss Goodson might possibly be softening?

His head shook the answer to all his questions regarding the appropriateness of his behavior. No. He must tell her. No matter what Mrs. Goodson thought. He would do it.

And then he began to respond to the invitations. All of them. Yes, he would go. He would step back into this society and do his duty as the marquis. And then, once the holidays were over, he would head to London. No one could fault him for that. The Season would be upon them. And with any luck, Miss Goodson would also be there.

And perhaps she wouldn't hate him.

When he got to the bottom of the stack, he saw a letter from Miss Goodson. He broke the seal and opened it quickly to read a lovely invitation, not to dine at her home, or to participate in any other frivolity, but to support the servants and the tenants in the main square in town on Boxing Day—December 26.

He rubbed a hand down his face.

Now here was a woman of quality. But wasn't it more the thing for the servants to be together on Boxing Day? Were the nobles even involved? He supposed for her festivity, they were. At least she seemed to hope others would attend or at least support. He rang his bell.

When a footman arrived, he handed him the invitation. "Would you please spread the word of this function? Let Cook and Mrs. Taylor particularly know that we will be supporting with our servants and tenants."

"Very good, my lord."

"And Jones?"

"Yes, my lord?"

"Thank you."

"You're most welcome."

He sat back in his chair. And then he rang the bell again.

Jones answered.

"Could you also alert Mrs. Taylor that we will be having a ball?"

If the footman was surprised, he gave no notion. Henry was rather impressed.

When Henry was again left to himself, he drummed his fingers on the desktop. Now, how to let Miss Goodson know before she found out in any other way?

To answer this question, he was at a loss, beyond simply telling her.

Perhaps he would do it on their sleigh ride. The more he thought about it, the more positive he felt that he would enjoy the sleigh and then before he returned her to her home, he would admit all.

He nodded, feeling slightly relieved from his growing guilt

the more he thought about it. To make certain he followed through, he penned an invitation to her grandmother.

"To our esteemed friends Mrs. Goodson and Miss Goodson,

It would give me the greatest satisfaction and enjoyment if I might come by tomorrow morning in my sleigh so that we could experience the beauty of the snow together."

Another servant was sent to deliver the invitation that moment.

He breathed out, and some of the tightness in his chest released. "Now we shall accept whatever consequences come."

He spent the rest of the day working on his shipping company, answering questions there, reviewing the books and preparing for his steward, who would come visit later that week. Every news he received of the business showed growth and success. So far, he could only be pleased.

The more he thought about it, the more intrigued he became with the idea of the silk that was made right here in Cheshire. He'd been shipping silk as part of his imports from the East Indies. But they were prohibited or largely restricted in England. The country had made it illegal to import the silks. But to learn that so much was made right here in his neighborhood, and some particularly by friends, he could only feel encouraged by the idea of using the local factories.

He made his way back out to the main parts of his home, determined to pay a visit to the silk factories in that moment. The towering walls, the portraits, the window dressings, all of it reminded him so clearly of his parents. He loved the connection, but he also longed for something new, something totally separate, something that didn't remind him of all that he'd missed. He knew London would provide that. But he needed the changes here at home as well. He thought of the greenery they'd collected. Decorating for Christmas would aid in the novelty and set new traditions.

He wondered how it would be appropriate for Miss Goodson

to join him in the decorating of his home. It would certainly be acceptable if her grandmother joined them. But first he would need to admit to her who he was. The complications of his plan gave him a headache, and he was again grateful for his planned sleigh ride in which to tell her all. He took a parting glance at a portrait of his father and then turned from the great hall. It was time to do some silk research.

He used the carriage to visit the silk factories. They sat just outside of town and were near one another. His wheels were newly tightened and were large enough to be able to make their way in the snow.

He stepped in the rather large and loud warehouse-like building. He assumed by the machines and the children running about that the building he was in did the weaving. He was fascinated to watch as strands were woven in and out of others, the makings of a beautiful, finished fabric at the end.

After a moment, a man approached him. "How might we help you, sir?"

"Yes, I'm Lord Wilmington. I'm interested in your silk."

"To purchase for a friend? We have shops and other locations in which to buy our many fine fabrics."

"Oh no, I'm interested in the reselling and shipping of your products."

The man's eyebrows rose for a moment and then he nodded. "Excellent. I shall let Mr. Farmington know you are here. Please follow me."

That was a good beginning, at any rate. Perhaps they could work out an arrangement. If Henry could get their silks to more places, perhaps they would sell it to him at a lower cost. Building this aspect of his business required he be in London. Another reason to hurry there filled him with an urgency, countered only by the need to be near Miss Goodson.

Her smile came to mind. She used her whole mouth. There was such a demure and gentle character about her until she smiled. And then her whole face transformed as though she were unable to contain the happiness.

He knew his grin grew just in the remembering. So much so that by the time he entered Mr. Farmington's office, he was surely smiling like a simpleton.

The man stood from behind his desk and eyed Henry curiously. "You're a cheerful sort of man, aren't you?"

"I am indeed." He cleared his throat. "Partly because I'm so pleased with everything I see here. I believe we can work well together for our mutual gain."

Mr. Farmington shook his hand. "Please sit, my lord. You have my full attention."

CHAPTER 15

*O*dette walked through town, a satchel full of invitations to the Boxing Day Festival slung on her shoulder. It was becoming a whole town gathering, and she was as pleased as could be. Though there appeared to be some confusion about whether or not the noble families would attend, they were at least highly generous in gifts and food for the day.

She stopped in the Hughes' store. No one was in the front room. "Hello," she called out, and then walked along the row of beautiful silks to see if anything new had arrived.

"Oh, Miss Goodson. We have your fabric ready."

"My fabric?"

"Yes, from the other day. It is real special, this one. You can't find it anywhere else in all of England." Mrs. Hughes held out a gorgeous shade of blue.

"Is this what you were twisting the other day?"

"Some of it is, yes. Do you like it?"

"Oh, it's exquisite. I've never seen such a lovely shade, nor felt such a delicious touch to a fabric. Can you imagine this in a dress?"

JEN GEIGLE JOHNSON

"Yes, on you, miss." Mrs. Hughes wrapped it in brown paper. "We need to get our seamstresses working on this for you."

"Yes, and come up with a good design as well."

"Certainly." She finished wrapping and then rested her arms on the counter, leaning forward. "Everyone's talking about Boxing Day. It's a beautiful thing you're doing."

"Thank you."

"We like it so much, the shop owners are adding to the day."

"You are?" Odette smiled.

"We are. We're going to come with booths and our wares and games to play."

Her heart lifted even higher. "Oh, that's excellent."

"And we're inviting local townships to come join us."

"Goodness. This is becoming quite the thing, isn't it?" She hugged her package to her chest.

"It is. And it will be good for us all, mark my words."

They discussed a few more of the details, and Odette left more grateful than ever for such a beautiful town full of caring people. This event was going to be much grander than she'd ever planned. If she were being honest, it was perhaps even more grand than she would like. What she wanted was the feeling of family at Christmas. But this would definitely fill in numbers of friends she cared about.

She exited the shop and made her way to the tearoom.

As soon as she entered, she wished she could turn and leave, but Miss Fenningway called out, "Oh, Miss Goodson."

And so she joined the two sisters sitting at a table in the middle of the room. They had tea spread out in front of them, including crumpets, clotted cream, cakes, and bits of cheeses. "This is wonderful. Thank you," Odette said.

She thought that perhaps the conversation would even be pleasing until Miss Eliza giggled. "Lord Wilmington is the absolute dream."

Miss Fenningway fanned her face. "He is, to be sure, don't you think, Miss Goodson?"

She was loathe to admit it, but what could she do? "I don't know all that much about him."

The two dropped open their mouths in unison. It might have been amusing, but Odette was not feeling overly prone to humor at the moment.

"I think I saw you together, though." Miss Fenningway narrowed her eyes. "I'm quite sure of it."

"Perhaps we were together and I didn't know it."

They burst into laughter. "And how could that ever happen? Everyone knows the marquis," Miss Fenningway said.

"Well, not everyone. How would I know him? He's been gone for large amounts of time. And well, I have been too." She was suddenly defensive about her lack of knowledge about the marquis.

"Oh, don't worry. I'm certain you will meet him. Have you received the invitation to the ball, at least?" Miss Eliza grinned. "I'm going to wear red. I know it's daring. But I wish to feel festive." She sniffed and raised her chin.

"I think that's a lovely choice." Had Odette received her invitation? Not to her knowledge. But the marquis wouldn't leave her and Grandmother off the invitation list, surely.

"At any rate, he's the most wonderful man of my acquaintance, and certainly of the area," Miss Eliza said.

"Too true. I've not met anyone as remotely wonderful as our marquis," Miss Fenningway agreed.

"And what a sense of humor."

"And such a giving sort of man. He will be kind, that is for certain."

Odette shifted in discomfort. "And how do you know him so well?"

"He's come to call." They shared a glance and then shrugged.

"We've been to his house for dinner." Eliza's eyes gleamed while she bragged.

"And we seem to run into him in all the places we go. We were quite hoping he would show up here." Miss Fenningway looked pointedly at the fourth and empty chair at their table.

"Do you think he will?" Odette searched the entryway and door to the tea shop.

"Who can say? He does tend to make an appearance wherever we are. We've taken to joking that he has an interest in one of us."

Miss Eliza sniffed again. "I'm certain we know who."

"As we've discussed, one can never know the inner workings of a man's heart. And until he declares himself, we are left in the dark."

"Except that he brought me the tart."

"We were all sitting at tea, Eliza. You were the closest. That hardly counts."

"He could just as easily have done the same for you, but he didn't." She looked away. "I think it must say something that he chose me in that moment."

"If he cares enough to declare himself, then we will know."

Odette could see that this was an old, tired conversation that might not end. She interrupted. "And is he handsome?" Where had that question come from? It wasn't even what she most wanted to know. But it certainly worked to distract the other two.

"Oh, handsome doesn't even begin to describe him." Miss Fenningway brought out her fan again.

"He has the most attentive eyes. They see into your soul."

"And his dark hair is just so thick and has the smallest amount of curl."

"He wears his clothing just right and he smiles out the corner of his mouth." Miss Eliza made her own crooked smile, perhaps in imitation of Lord Wilmington.

He sounded familiar to Odette, even almost quite a bit like Mr. Wardlow. "How tall is he?"

"He's tall. I stand at his shoulder," Miss Fenningway said.

"No, we are more at his chest."

"I thought him shorter, so that I can almost see into his eyes when next to him."

Miss Eliza shrugged. "I guess we don't really know."

"I find it odd that his boots have scratches and his jacket is older." Miss Fenningway closed her fan. "But who can blame him? He's just returned from the East Indies."

Odette's breathing picked up. She'd not thought of it before, but had Mr. Wardlow and Lord Wilmington known each other? They were sounding very similar. A hole of apprehension opened up inside her as dread built. She'd spoken so harshly of Lord Wilmington, and Mr. Wardlow had often come to his defense. They were certainly friends. They'd skated on the marquis's pond, hadn't they? Suddenly, as a friend to Mr. Wardlow, all her previous complaints of a distant person she'd never met felt personal and close to home, and she became rather ashamed. "He seems like a truly good sort of person, then."

"Oh he is. The kindest eyes." Miss Fenningway nodded. "You can tell that about a man, you know."

Odette did know, and all she could think about was Mr. Wardlow. Was he to be the standard of every good man for her? Disturbed by her previous prejudice, she asked, "And you found no . . . neglectful pride in him? No evidence of a man who would disregard a mother's funeral?"

Miss Eliza shook her head emphatically. "Oh, certainly not. One cannot travel quickly from the East Indies, you know." Her chin rose with superiority. "He did in fact look a bit haunted by it."

Odette wilted in her seat. It took effort to remain upright. She'd judged him so harshly, so very wrongly. "And you feel he might even now be suffering from his loss?"

"Oh certainly. The man wears grey. But more than that, he is absolutely haunted by the responsibility all around him." Miss Fenningway spoke with full authority. And Odette could do naught but believe her.

The shame of her own thoughts and words descended. She would need to make it up to him. In fact, she recognized she and Grandmother had a responsibility to their neighbor that they had very much neglected. None of Cook's tarts were dropped off to welcome him home. No dinner invitations were extended to him. Nothing was said or done to indicate that she and Grandmother were especially kind or attentive neighbors either. She sat back as the two sisters continued to expound on the marquis's many fine qualities. And all she could think about was her true neglect and errant thoughts where he was concerned.

Should she seek a courtship as Grandmother wished? No, not with a man like Mr. Wardlow in her life. But should she be a better person to this stranger? She certainly should.

She vowed that even that very evening, she would drop by a basket herself, with a card inviting him over to dine.

CHAPTER 16

$\mathcal{H}$enry was pleased with his conversations at the silk factories. Their potential partnership was exciting, and could be very profitable. He'd sent letters off to his solicitor to draw up contractual paperwork with that in mind. And now, he was heading into the opposite side of town, where he hoped to buy Miss Goodson a gift. His steps were light. The snow was still falling, and everything was covered in white. A slow whistle escaped his lips without even planning it. "God Rest Ye Merry Gentlemen" kept his steps light and his mood happy.

He'd buy her something small, for Christmas. A memento, perhaps, though he'd like to buy much more. One day he would, he hoped. The coming admission of his true identity eased his guilt as well as increased his angst. The blue silk was on his mind as well as a certain other shop.

Despite the falling snow, their small row of shops was bustling with people. He realized with pleasant surprise that he was acquainted with many of them. Knowing the families of the people his parents knew and loved gave the whole town a comfortable feeling. And even though he'd spent little time with the people in this town, he had come home for Christmas now

115

and again, and they were all now a part of his feelings of nostalgia for the beauty of the season. He picked up his pace. Perhaps some ribbon? He stepped inside the first store, suddenly the only man in a cluster of pretty skirts. Every eye turned to him immediately and the room grew quiet for a half a breath, and then increasingly louder as four groups of women approached.

The first to arrive, the Fenningways, took possession of both his elbows. Eliza stood unreasonably close, but the shop was crowded, after all. "Oh, Lord Wilmington. We are so happy you've come. We're all here to pick out ribbons for your ball."

"For my ball? All of you?"

Many heads in the room nodded.

And so he followed suit, a slow sort of understanding coming through in the lowering and raising of his head. "Then I wish you the best." He grinned, unsure what was expected of him, and at once wishing to retreat. He would certainly not be buying ribbon.

"But do tell us, if you know. What are the colors?" Miss Eliza asked.

"Colors?"

"Yes, how will you be decorating? Your centerpieces, or the dishes, anything."

Henry was flummoxed. He had no notion that these sorts of things were even discussed. He imagined that perhaps his house-keeper would know the answer to their question. But really, did a host choose a color theme? Did the ladies hope to match it? Some social niceties were a complete puzzle to him. He had nothing to tell them, but their eyes, open and hopeful, were waiting for some-thing, anything from him. He cleared his throat. "Blue, perhaps?"

The ladies all bustled closer to the row of blue.

He dipped his head. "Perhaps I shall wander about a bit on this side of the store?" He gestured away to the very opposite side, where the yellow ribbons seemed to reside.

The Fenningways seemed torn. Did they make their way to his side or stay put to make certain they were able to purchase the amount of blue ribbon required?

As he moved in the opposite direction, they soon relinquished his arms and hurried over to join the crowd now grasping for multiple shades of blue.

He breathed out one long breath and then turned to the far wall. What he really hoped was that this store carried things other than ribbons. As he made his way and turned a corner, he was rewarded with a row of curious cylinders. He leaned over the case, trying to make out their identity.

"Music boxes." A man behind the counter pointed down toward the general location. "You wind them up and they play music back to you. Made in Switzerland."

"Now that is something." He at once wanted to gift one to Miss Goodson, but knew it to be much too grand a gift.

The shopkeeper reached in and took one out. "Here, I'll show you." He turned a key at the back of the device that fit in his hand. After the soft sounds of a cranking noise, he straightened again, and a melody came from the box. The familiar three-count beat made Henry smile. "Is that a waltz?"

"It is indeed. You can have your own waltz anytime you like." The shopkeeper wiggled his eyebrows. "Thinking more for the misses, of course. I'm unsure your situation." The man studied him.

"I'm Lord Wilmington."

"Ah, pardon me, my lord. But perhaps you could save it for when you might have a use for it?"

Henry nodded. "Very good. Please wrap it up."

"Excellent choice, if I do say so."

"Thank you. Now, I'm needing something smaller, a token, a trinket."

The shopkeeper nodded. "I have just the thing."

Henry felt, without even yet seeing, bodies near him. Listening ears, curious eyes.

"On second thought, I'll take the one package and perhaps return another day."

"Excellent, my lord." The man wrapped his box and tied it tightly, then Henry thanked him and eased his way around the women in the shop and out the door.

Perhaps some might have followed him, but he'd been introduced to only a few of that particular bunch. How could one town have so many eligible young ladies?

He resisted stretching out his arms and loosening his cravat, and continued down the street. Perhaps he'd purchase some crumpets and cakes before returning.

"Is that Mr. Wardlow?" Miss Goodson's pleased-sounding voice was a balm to his semi-troubled ears.

He turned, not even attempting to dim his smile. "And how are you, Miss Goodson?"

"I'm well! Now that I've seen you, very well. The snow has not let up, has it?"

"Not one bit, and I can't say that I have it in me to complain. We are all capable of being out in it, it seems. We've made it into town. What more could a person want from a snow?"

"I don't know. It's the kind of snow I wish to look upon for hours."

Henry held out his arm. "I too. And tell me, where might I escort you?"

"I've just come from purchasing ribbons." She shook her head.

"Have you?"

"Yes, and you'll never guess."

"I don't think I could." He winced inside.

"There is a literal mob in that store on the blue ribbons."

"The blue, you say?"

"Yes, and might I tell you why?"

118

"I'm not able to feel at ease until you do."

"The marquis has disclosed that there will be blue at his ball." Miss Goodson smiled triumphantly.

He studied her. Was she not completely annoyed at this new desire to please the marquis?

She held up a bag.

His mouth dropped open. "And so you bought some?"

"I did. I bought yards and yards . . . of red!" She laughed.

And he joined her, for some reason relieved she had not fallen prey to the frantic desires to present herself in just such a way to the marquis. "Very well done. You shall be the only one in red, then?"

"It appears so." She shook her head. "But I've come to think I've been dreadfully mistaken about the marquis."

Henry nearly stumbled. "How so? He's not the ogre you've imagined?"

"Not at all. You tried to tell me. I can see it clearly now. He is a good enough sort of person, isn't he?"

"He is indeed."

"And you. I understand you're friends. How do you know him?"

"Oh, me. Know him. Yes, well, I . . ." His mind froze. How did he know him? Or himself? How did Mr. Wardlow know the marquis?

When he didn't answer right away, she continued. "I mean, I've always assumed you were raised here together—of course you'd know each other. Perhaps at school?" She paused, but not long enough to give an answer, thankfully. He didn't relish lying to her. So far, he'd not had to. She continued, filling in information in answer to her own question.

Before she could ramble on forever without him, he placed a hand over hers. "I'm happy to hear you give our marquis a bit of grace."

She nodded. "I do feel I've been too harsh. When I realized

he was a friend of yours, he became all the more personal. I apologize."

He swallowed twice before he was able to speak in a normal voice. She was too good. And now she'd apologized, when he was the one to need to do so. Would this woman ever forgive him? "Please, Miss Goodson. You must not apologize. Who knows but your impressions were accurate? I believe everyone makes mistakes. And it is likely that our dear marquis might regret the time away from his mother for the rest of his life." He had to stop speaking for the emotion that suddenly welled in his throat.

But thankfully, she still had much to say. "Oh I know, and I do feel dreadful for him at the same time that I wish he'd been here. There is just so much good he could do." Her nose wrinkled as she seemed to be considering a great many things. And he was enchanted by her sweet face.

"I don't imagine you would ever do such a thing, desert your family and friends in the pursuit of success and wealth, Miss Goodson. There are people who are veritable angels in disguise. And I believe you are one of those. And then, unfortunately, there are the rest of us." Henry placed a hand over hers. "Thank you for your patience with the rest of us mere mortals."

She waved her hand in the air. "Oh tosh, angel indeed. I'm really nothing more than a woman looking for community, for family." She looked away, and he could see hints of an emotional struggle in her face.

"Tell me."

She shook her head. "It is too tender at the moment." She brushed her cheek. "Forgive me."

He allowed her a moment to compose herself, picking back up his whistle.

"Oh, that has become one of my favorite carols." She blew out through pursed lips. "But I'm afraid I cannot whistle."

"Then you must learn." He pursed his lips. "It is all about the shape of your mouth, and your tongue."

Her cheeks colored. "My tongue?"

"Yes, certainly. I'm afraid I cannot show you, but if you imagine my tongue is back behind my lips, framing a similar shape and lower against my bottom teeth, then you can see what a tongue does." He whistled again, contemplating his mouth. "However, no one ever told me these things. I watched others, practiced, and one day it just stuck. Perhaps it's best not to over-think such things."

She nodded. "Then I shall do the same, if you wouldn't mind whistling?"

"Of course. I stopped, didn't I?" He began again with "God Rest Ye Merry Gentlemen." And it required a certain amount of concentration with her new attentive stare at his mouth. But he was soon distracted by her own attempts. At first, she breathed out way too quickly. Then, of course, too slowly. For a moment, he thought she might faint from so much breath coming in and out of her mouth.

But at last, as they reached the end of the lane, a small sound exited her lips.

"You've done it!" He watched her closely as she tried again. This time, the sound came louder. "Excellent. Most excellent." He listened. "Keep at it. You must do it enough that you can repeat the attempt later. Then I expect some practicing to make you proficient."

She nodded in response, keeping her lips pursed just so, and blowing out to make the breathy sound she'd managed.

They paused as they reached the end of the shops. With nowhere to go, he didn't want to end their time together. "Would you care for some tea or a stop by the bakery?"

"Oh, both would be lovely." She grinned then gasped. "Oh no, I've stopped whistling." She pursed her lips again and the same sound exited.

"You've done it. Now you will always be able to whistle."

"You think so?"

"Most definitely. You've taught yourself. The next step is to make a melody, to whistle a song."

She held her chin up, her steps coming along lighter. "I'm quite proud of myself."

He laughed into the sky. "As you should be." He placed a hand over hers again on his arm, and then led them back down the street. "Come, let's get you warmed up."

"Why don't you entertain?" she asked suddenly.

"Pardon?"

"You don't have dinners. I don't hear people speaking of you. Forgive me, but never. And I don't know where you live." She stopped and turned her lovely face up to his.

Heaven help him, he didn't know what to say. "Well, I . . ." He closed his mouth. "I don't know."

"Do you live near town?"

"I think we've talked about my estate, haven't we?"

She started to shake her head.

"No, I'm sure of it. We have."

They began walking again, with Miss Goodson's face drawn and puzzled beside him.

"But since you don't recall, I live outside of town. I have an estate. I . . . entertain. But I'm also slightly uncomfortable doing so, as I don't live with anyone else."

She tilted her head to the side. "And your parents?"

"They have both since passed." Would she just discover on her own that he was the marquis? He felt his face heat.

"You are so identical to the marquis."

Henry coughed. "Pardon me?"

"You both are so similar. I'm surprised I didn't see it before."

"Oh, well, I . . ."

"It's what made me realize that you're friends. And that he is a real person, and I best be more kind." She shrugged. "Thank you for that."

"You're welcome. But dear Miss Goodson, you are not in need of so much apology. Come. Let us warm and cheer ourselves in the tearoom."

They entered and all eyes again turned to them. Most of the women from the ribbon store had moved to the tearoom. And that's when he realized his mistake.

CHAPTER 17

"$\mathcal{M}$iss Goodson, perhaps we might go to the bakery first instead?" Mr. Wardlow's eyes darted around the room and returned to her, almost as if he were nervous.

"Certainly. It's rather crowded in here, isn't it?"

"Yes, quite." He turned and pushed open the door again, practically running from the shop.

"Goodness, yes, it was rather warm as well. I quite enjoy the chill if I've the clothes for it."

"As do I. And more than tea, I find I need some gingerbread, sweet cakes, bread, even crumpets."

She laughed. "You are one who enjoys his sweets, then?"

"Yes, are you?" His hopeful, almost boyish expression cheered her again.

"I do. I admit to being quite partial to gingerbread."

"Mm, yes, I can see why you would be. The smell alone is enough to make one start a craving."

The room was far less crowded, and the counter was open. Behind the glass were all manner of lovely things to eat. She peered closer at a row of what looked like tarts. "And what are these?"

"Oh, those are our new custards. It's Christmas pudding in the center there," the baker said.

"That sounds most delicious. I've never heard of that."

"It's completely new. We attempted it the other evening when practicing for the Christmas treats we will start filling our shelves with."

"And it was a success?"

"We like to think so, but we recommend you see for yourself." The man winked, and Odette was shocked for a moment, but saw that he was just all in fun.

Mr. Wardlow spoke in quiet tones to the other person behind the counter, and then he turned. "We should both choose whichever treats we want to taste now and to bring home to our tables." He gestured with his hand. "Please, it is my treat."

"Thank you." Odette found that she had quite a taste for sweets as well. But conscious that someone else was paying, she asked for some gingerbread to bring home, and for the Christmas pudding tart to try in the store. "I'm quite intrigued by this idea right here."

"I as well. We better make that two, one for me as well."

They carried their goodies to a corner table. Odette took a long, slow bite. The custard center filled her mouth with a sweet, cool, slightly spice-filled goodness. "This is delicious. I can see why they decided to begin selling such a delectable thing."

Mr. Wardlow's eyes had not left her face.

She chewed slowly, suddenly aware of every movement of her mouth. When she looked away, he rested his hand over top hers. "Forgive me. I find the sight of you enjoying that morsel to be difficult to resist."

She raised a hand to her cheek. "Oh?" The smile that followed could not be helped.

Mr. Wardlow's handsome, perceptive eyes noticed, of course. Then he tried his own bite, and his eyes closed in pure enjoyment. She'd never seen someone appreciate a bite of food so much. But when he opened his eyes again, and they were full of teasing, she knew he was overly dramatizing.

"Did I behave in such a way? Is that why you tease?"

"Not at all. You were the real, authentic beauty. I was a mere copy. In truth, I simply wanted to see if you would enjoy the sight as much as I had."

She felt her cheeks flame again, but she rallied. "I, of course, could never know."

"Too true." He dabbed his mouth. "And now we must talk about more important things."

"Than tarts?"

"Even than tarts. Our sleigh ride. Will you be prepared for such a thing?"

"Oh yes, Grandmother and I are equally excited. Thank you for thinking of us."

He peered toward the door. "I do think the snow has paused. Though I'm certain there is enough on the ground for the sleigh to behave quite nicely."

"Grandmother said she'd like to join us for but a moment. She said her bones are complaining of the cold, but that we might continue for longer, should we wish."

"I appreciate that trust. And I shall make sure we have plenty of warming stones and blankets and furs."

"How thoughtful. That would be lovely. I worry so for her." Odette hadn't allowed the thoughts to linger, but Grandmother seemed to be more tired and less active, and certainly kept to herself more. Odette hoped she was not in pain, or not too much.

"Is she well?"

"I don't know. She complains of her bones. And she's slowing down. I'm doing most of the holiday preparations, as well as the inviting and responding to invitations. We are keeping mostly to ourselves." She didn't like that. But how could she complain? She had the entire town gathering for the Boxing Day celebrations. She would have plenty of people at her side.

Or so she told herself. But she knew no matter how many people she gathered around her, no one would ever replace her parents. And that was just something that she would have to face head-on one of these years.

Mr. Wardlow pulled a timepiece from his pocket. "And how are you getting home?"

"I have the carriage and my maid waiting somewhere hereabouts."

"Oh, pity." He grinned. "But I shall see you this afternoon. Come, shall I walk you to them?"

"Yes, thank you. I believe I'm finished here."

They both gathered their packages and he opened the door. A group of ladies eyed them and pointed from far down at the other end of the street. Did Odette imagine things, or did Mr. Wardlow groan?

"They are very social today." She watched them as they hurried forward.

"I cannot fathom what has them so excitable."

Her carriage pulled forward.

"But here you go. I'll find my own and look forward to the beauty of the quiet snow in amongst all the pine trees between our two estates." He sucked in a breath.

But she was so focused on a rather frenzied approach of women that she hardly paid attention. "I'll enjoy the trees almost more than anything." For a moment, their faces were close, their breath mingled, and then she allowed him to help her up into the carriage. "Thank you for this enjoyable afternoon."

"You're welcome." He peered into her carriage. "See you soon."

As the carriage pulled away, she placed a hand on her heart. "Oh help. He is almost too much for me." The pounding was delicious. She tore off her gloves and fanned her face.

Her maid remained expressionless, and Odette was pleased not to have to explain herself. She peered back out the window just as the women approached. "Oh! Lord Wilmington!" someone called from the back of the group. Odette craned her neck further out. Would she at last catch a glimpse of the famed marquis?

But they were now moving too far away. And the group seemed to be made up of Mr. Wardlow and the women only. She would have to see him another day.

In fact, were they not invited to dinner and the ball in the next week? And then, of course, there was Christmas Eve, Boxing Day, then Twelfth Night. She busied her mind with making preparations for all three until she arrived home.

"Grandmother!" she called into the house. Perhaps that was not the most couth thing to do. She knew her grandmother might not be too pleased either. She turned to their butler. "Where is Grandmother?"

"She has retired to her rooms, miss."

"Oh?" Odette handed off her outer things quickly and rushed up the stairs. The closed door to her grandmother's rooms felt ominously shut, not just comfortably so. But she tapped on the door and then peered in. "Grandmother?"

The room was dark, and smelled of healing herbs. "Are you well?"

"Come in, yes, I just need a bit of rest." Her voice was tired and came from the dark shadows of her bed.

Odette tiptoed closer, remembering all too well a similar view of her parents' beds. But as she neared, she was relieved to see her grandmother sitting up in bed. "I'm well enough, but my head aches, and the dark is comforting."

"The room is warm."

"Yes, the chill is hard on my bones as well."

"Perhaps next year, we go somewhere with less of a chill?"

"Yes, perhaps." Grandmother's voice sounded far away again. "Tell me about your walk into town."

"Oh, it was lovely. I purchased gingerbread and cakes at the bakery. Well, that is to say, Mr. Wardlow did. He means it as a gift to us."

Grandmother's smile was warm, almost tender.

"You do like him, don't you?" Odette asked.

"I like him very much. I hope that you will too."

"Oh I do. And he seems to be most interested. What will I do if he wishes to court me?"

"Isn't he already?"

She thought about their interactions and then nodded. "It does appear so, but he's said nothing."

"Not all men must declare their courtship. And perhaps he did so to me and I kept it to myself."

Odette gasped. But then when her grandmother's body was shaking in laughter, she let it go. "We talked of the sleigh ride. Shall I tell him to come another day?"

"No, no, child. You two go ahead. I need the rest, and you need the outing."

"I'm sorry you're unwell. Will you . . . recover?" She asked what she most feared and clenched her hands together quietly in her lap, the silence evidence of her concern.

"I believe so. I am most in need of rest, I believe. And warmer weather. As I get those two things, I will most definitely improve."

"Then perhaps it would be better for us in London."

"I do believe it will be. But of course, we must travel in order to get to London. I cannot be traveling quite yet. And Odette, I've been meaning to tell you. Don't miss out on social events because of your old grandmother. I've asked Mrs. Fenningway if you might attend different parties with them. What do you think of that?"

Odette didn't know what to think. "Of course that will be fine. I wish I would be with you though. You're family. You are the one I most cherish."

"Thank you, dear. I feel the same about you. But some of

these events, they aren't for your grandmother anyway. And Mrs. Fenningway can chaperone you with her girls just as much as anyone."

"Thank you. And Boxing Day?"

"Are you set on attending?"

"I am."

"I might need to send you with another. I'm sorry. That kind of energy might not be available in these tired limbs."

Odette nodded. "Thank you, though, for letting me plan it and for the gifts we are giving."

"Of course. I love to see you so involved, so caring of others. I hear the marquis has his staff supporting the event. They reached out to our servants. I believe he might feed half the village."

Odette sucked in a breath. "Is he really helping? That much?"

"It sounds like it. Maybe he will finally show his face where we can see him, and the two of you will be introduced."

"Perhaps. That would be nice, I think."

'You think?"

"Well, I've thought ill of him for so long, I do believe I might feel guilty when I see him."

Grandmother laughed. "I don't know if that is what you will feel. But I'm certain you'll feel something."

"What do you mean by that?"

She waved away Odette's question. "For now, we must only ask ourselves, have we seen him already and not known who he was?"

Odette considered her. "I suppose that is possible. Everyone in the whole place seems to have met him but me."

"What if he was behind you or at your side, any number of times? What if you have spoken to him?" Grandmother wiggled her eyebrows, then leaned her head back against the wall.

Odette knew she needed to leave her grandmother in peace. "Who can know? But I've decided to like him."

"You have?"

"Yes, he and Mr. Wardlow are friends. He's a real, living being, and I've been unfair."

"That is very mature of you. I'm proud to be your grandmother." She held Odette's hand in her own soft ones. Odette had often thought that her grandmother had the softest hands in the world.

Her voice grew quieter and Odette leaned in closer to hear. "I remember the marquis when he was just a lad." She paused, and Odette thought she'd fallen asleep, but then her words continued. "He was the most generous lad. We had a group of village children and they wanted to start up a school. We thought about sending you, do you remember?"

"A little bit, yes. Was the marquis around then?"

"He was, but you were too old for such things, and we had already registered you for Fanny L'Entre's. We did the right thing. But perhaps you would have crossed paths then, had you stayed. He was on his way to Eton, of course. But he went to the school, mostly to help the other children. And stayed late tutoring many of them."

"Oh, that's so surprising. Most wouldn't do that, would they?"

Grandmother shook her head. "You would. But you're correct, I believe most would not have done such a thing, largely because people are so set on mingling with only people like them." She smiled. "But we already know you don't have that same restriction. Nor does he, apparently."

"Or he didn't then."

"True. Another time, I was walking home from the market. I'd purchased a bag of apples. They had just arrived, and I knew our housekeeper wouldn't be there in time enough to snatch up a few. But on the way, the bag was so heavy and I dropped it, apples spilling everywhere. But of course, Lord Wilmington arrived shortly after, picked up my apples, and carried them back home with me." She sighed. "Good boy." When she didn't say more for several moments, Odette knew she was asleep.

"Mr. Wardlow was so odd today. Do we really know him?" Of course, Grandmother didn't respond. Odette stood and kissed the dear woman on the cheek. "Rest well. Shall I ask the servants to deliver anything?"

Her eyes fluttered open. "No, I'm fine. Just some rest. Thank you." She drifted back off to sleep.

Odette slipped away as quietly as she could with much to think of. Had she met the marquis? She didn't think it would be possible to meet him and not know who he was, not from what everyone had said about him.

At any rate, she was looking forward to her sleigh ride. She entered her room, calling for her maid. Perhaps she would pay extra attention to her appearance.

CHAPTER 18

*W*hen Henry arrived back home, he was greeted almost immediately by his steward, Mr. Hansen. "My lord, forgive the intrusion, but we've received news."

"It must be important news indeed."

"Yes, it is my opinion that it merits immediate attention."

"Excellent. Let's convene in the study, then, shall we?" Henry handed the purchases to his butler and led the way toward that part of the house. The closer he moved to the study, the more he became completely engrossed in his business. What had happened? He loosened his cravat. The sounds of the East Indies echoed in the ears of his memory, pulling him into the times where all he did was build his shipping business. He almost forgot the steward was at his heels. But the man shut the door and got right to the point. "Your captain on the *Marauder* has quit."

"Quit? Was there trouble? Why did he quit?"

"Apparently some disagreement with the purser, and the two couldn't mend things. The captain refuses to have him aboard."

"Can we not find another purser?" Henry brought a hand to his forehead.

"Apparently he is also the supercargo."

"Ah, much more difficult to replace." He groaned. "But not as difficult as the captain. What has been done to win him back? He cannot just walk away. Captain Grey is the best there is. I know. I have wined and wooed that fellow until I had liquor coming out my ears."

"Nothing has been done. Everyone is looking to you to bring him back and soothe ruffled pride."

What he heard from his steward was concerning indeed. He needed Captain Grey. He needed a captain, any captain, in order to sail, but he needed Captain Grey if he were to run his shipping business the way he wanted. And his steward was correct. The best thing for Henry's business was for him to leave that moment and spend the rest of the holidays in London, with frequent visits to the shipyard and to his sellers and buyers. But he hesitated.

The steward had been gone these thirty minutes past, and yet, Henry waited. He did not immediately call for a servant to pack his trunks.

Instead, he thought of Miss Goodson. After many more minutes, he stood. "Perhaps I shall go on that sleigh ride now." He spoke to no one in particular. The room was empty except for him.

But as he exited, a host of servants stood ready.

"Hello, thank you. I don't believe I will be traveling, as you might have heard. We will continue as before. I find I would like to stay here in Cheshire for the holiday. But perhaps we could be ready to depart at any moment, and certainly after Twelfth Night."

"Very good, my lord." His valet bowed and stepped away down the hall.

Henry followed. "And I'll be needing the sleigh pulled up front."

"Very good, my lord." A footman left in the direction of the door leading to the stables.

His mind full of business, Miss Goodson, and oddly at once, his father, Henry prepared himself for what he hoped would be an important afternoon with Miss Goodson. He and the valet took extra care. He dabbed some waters on himself as well.

He exited, patted his jacket pockets, and then made his way to the sleigh, trusting that his servants had prepared everything according to his directions.

WHEN THE SLEIGH pulled up in front of her house, Odette rested a hand at her stomach. All of her insides seemed to be in a flutter at once, and she was unsure if she enjoyed the sensation, or if it made her nervous. Probably both. But one thing she knew: The sleigh ride would be most enjoyable. She laughed as Mr. Wardlow leapt down, his top hat and red scarf reminding her of the first day they'd met. He had a vibrancy she'd not seen in anyone else. He stood tall; every time she saw him, she noticed how tall he was. His eyes sparkled in a way that lit the air around him. She asked the butler to open the door. Just as he raised a hand to knock, he was standing in front of her with nothing between them. "Hello." He bowed.

"Mr. Wardlow." She curtseyed low and lifted her lashes slowly. "I'm looking forward to our afternoon."

When she stepped out the door instead of inviting him in, he craned his neck around her. "Is your grandmother ready as well?"

"She is not joining us. Her latest bouts of illness have kept her in bed today."

"Oh, I'm sorry to hear that. Perhaps there is more we can do for her. Has a doctor been called?"

"She mentioned she has been seeing him, yes."

"Very good."

"And she assures me that she will recover. She thinks it's a mild malady."

"I suppose she would know, but if she is as stubborn a soul as I, and she won't seek out what is best for her, please allow me to assist. I can fetch the doctor, send healing poultices, whatever might be required."

"Thank you." Odette warmed further at his great thoughtfulness. "Tell me more about how you know my grandparents."

He held out his arm. "That I would love to do, while we are in the sleigh." He led her to a remarkable, carriagelike equipage with sleigh blades for wheels.

"You've decorated!" She grinned. Greenery ran from front to back, and ribbons tied in bows added more to the festivity. "It's lovely."

"I hoped you would enjoy it. Tomorrow is Christmas Eve."

"I cannot believe it, honestly. With grandmother being ill and me focused on Boxing Day, the holiday has snuck up on me."

"Well, we shall have to mark it right now, and take this time to celebrate." He assisted her up into her seat, then walked around the other side to join her.

"I see we have Ginger and Bread to join us again."

"Oh, yes. They were the most impatient in the barn."

"And have the most appropriate names."

"Too true. I don't know that we would feel quite the same riding with Sun and Flower."

She tried to hide her smile but could not. "Who named your horses? I must know."

"It was I—as a lad, mind you, but still I." He grinned unabashedly. "And they never deviated from those childlike names, bless them."

"You were loved."

"I absolutely was." He lifted the reins, and a delightful bell sounded in the air.

"You've added bells."

"Yes, I feel no sleigh ride can be complete without the sound of bells."

"They're a happy sound, full of hope." She appreciated the cheery, jolly atmosphere of their ride. It cleared some of her concern over her grandmother.

"I quite agree. The church bell, the sleigh bell, the bell pull."

Odette laughed. "The bell pull?"

"Certainly, anything we want is at the other end of that bell pull."

She considered Mr. Wardlow. She had never before thought about the implications of his words. "You are right. I'm astounded that I might pull the cord and have whatever I wish. I suppose I've never utilized our servants to their full capabilities."

"Or perhaps you are too good a soul to require undue effort on their part."

"Perhaps." She tucked her hands deeper inside her muff.

"Are you warm? We have the blankets. The blocks. Whatever you need."

"I'm quite warm, thank you." She moved just enough so that she felt him beside her. "This is nice."

"I quite agree with you there. I think I shall command Ginger and Bread to go as slowly as possible over our winter magic, shall I?"

"I would be pleased if our journeyings took the whole of the day. Go as slowly as you like."

His arm encircled her back, hand resting on her shoulder, while the other held the reins. "Then a slow, leisurely pace it is." He clucked his tongue, and the horses started to move.

Snow fell all around once again in thick, beautiful flakes. With sleigh blades riding over the top of any bumps in the road, they glided over the snow in a great and quiet calm. The only sounds were the occasional tinkle of the bells, the shaking of the harness and chains on the horses, their intermittent huffs into the air, and the slipping of their sleigh across the snow. It was all soothing to Odette, and she wished, just as she'd said, that she would be many hours thus.

"We must share our favorite Christmas memories," Mr. Wardlow said.

"Oh, that is a wonderful idea." Odette had been thinking of hers all last evening. She missed her parents every year. And this week most especially. "I came here when I was ten. So I was very young when my parents passed away, but some of my cherished memories are from the times when they were still alive. We lived far from here. And it rarely snowed, but one morning, right before Christmas, a thin dusting of snow fell all around us. Father and I were so excited, and anxious to get outside. I hoped to go sledding, to roll around in the great whiteness. Father hoped to . . ." She laughed. "I don't know what he hoped. At the time, I assumed he wanted everything I wanted." She shook her head, trying to capture all the details. "So we rushed to a hill, the smallest bit of incline, and sat at the top, hoping to get moving, that the smallest covering of white would be enough."

She laughed at the memory.

"And it wasn't?"

"Oh no. We started out, perhaps a few inches, and then stopped."

"A pity."

"But Father then did the most amazing thing. He leapt off and commenced rolling down the hill, shouting, 'You have to try this!' And so I did. Much to Mother's dismay, as my skirts were quite soiled."

"Oh, that's the most jolly story. Your father sounds like the good sort."

"Yes, he was. The good sort." She turned her chin up to see into his face. Mr. Wardlow was the good sort. There was quite a lot about him that reminded her of her father. "Your turn. I'm afraid mine are from my childhood."

"Then I shall share one more recent, though I have cherished

Christmas memories from childhood as well. I will share this past Christmas, as I believe it might have changed my life forever."

Odette sat very still, willing him to share as much as he could. She'd heard so little about his past, knew so little of the details of his life.

"I was in the heat of the sun. I know that doesn't sound much like what we are experiencing right now."

"Not at all. Did you even realize it was Christmas?"

"Not entirely. Very few around us celebrated the holiday. And there was work to be done. But I did pause to step into town and purchase cider. They had some for the East India Company men who would come into port, and it was just right for me. But as I was leaving, two little urchins tugged at my pant legs."

The story had taken an entirely different vein than she'd expected, but she was captivated.

"They had these huge brown eyes. They were dressed in rags and they couldn't have stood taller than my knees. So very young. In their hands were old crusts of bread. Dirty, as though trampled on from the road."

"Oh dear." Odette's heart went out to them, wherever they now were.

"Yes, and so I took them right back into that store and purchased whatever they wanted."

Delighted, she laughed. "And what did they want?"

"That's the most remarkable thing. They both wanted bread. Of course. They looked like they rarely ate a full meal. But then they each picked out sheaves of paper."

"How curious."

"Yes; turns out, it was for their mama, so she could write their papa and ask where he'd gone."

"Oh." Odette's heart went out to that family.

"Yes, he worked onboard an East Indiaman somewhere, and

they'd not heard from him nor received any money from him in many months."

"So what did you do?" She knew Mr. Wardlow had done something. He had to have.

"Well, I asked to follow them home and invited the mother to come with her two children and work in my house."

Odette gasped. "You are a saint!"

"No, I'm not, unfortunately. As you might discover. But I was happy that I had the means to help out this one family."

"And their father? Have you located him?"

"We are still searching, but it won't be too much longer. I only hope and pray that he was not lost at sea."

"Oh yes, that would be tragic for them, but at least they have the means to live on now. Where are they?"

"I left them there, in the East Indies. I think they will do better there, and besides, it turns out the woman is a fabulous organizer. She helps run my house."

She considered him. "Do you prefer it there?"

His eyes widened a moment and he hesitated before answering. "No."

"But?"

He looked away. "But it is lovely there. I would be conflicted if I lived there."

"Just like you are here."

He sighed. "I suppose."

But then he clicked the reins, and the horses picked up speed. "There's an excellent bit of field and space up here. Shall we see how fast our sleigh can go?"

"Oh yes." She leaned forward as the horses went ever faster, the wind refreshing on her cheeks. They raced over the land all around them, the world blurring into one grand landscape of white. And then the clouds parted up ahead, and a beautiful stream of sunshine lit the snow all around one spot. Flakes still fell. Sun glistened off the snow, and their bed became a sea of sparkling wonder. Everywhere Odette looked, diamonds glistened back. She raised a hand to her mouth and swiveled in her seat to see every angle. "This is enchanting."

Mr. Wardlow slowed the horses. Neither spoke a sound, the world around them shouting in silent splendor. Odette tried to capture it perfectly in her memory, but knew she never could. This experience was to be lived, to enjoy in the now, to grant them a moment of God's gifts. Mr. Wardlow reached for her hand. It seemed the most natural thing in the world, but as their fingers laced together, a great wholeness filled her. She turned to face him, the words "I love you" at the tip of her lips. Shocked at her feelings, amazed at the glorious scene around her, at the man to her front, she could only search his face. She daren't say the words to acknowledge what was happening in her heart. She daren't say any words.

He lifted a hand up to the side of her face and cradled her cheek. "Odette."

Her name, whispered from his lips, filled her with greater wonder even than what she saw all around them. "Mm," she murmured.

"I . . . there is something I must tell you. But you have captured my soul. I'm yours." He moved closer until their lips were close enough that she could feel the warmth of his without touching. Everything was a blur before her, but the air was filled with scents of him. His earthy essence entered her and stayed, everything expanding, her stomach clenching. Reaching for him without realizing it, she was in his arms, hers wrapped around him, their faces close, lips . . . brushing. Each touch of the softness of his mouth sent a cascade of tingles through her. A brief glimpse of what it would be like to be his and then stop. So much so that she shivered from craving more, always more, until she closed her eyes and his mouth covered hers—and stayed.

The world burst around her, in happy swirling thoughts that would not rest in one place to notice. He pressed again and again. His arms tightened around her and she wished to be closer, ever closer. But she was overwhelmed. She paused for air, and then laughed, kissing him again and again. "That was . . ." She turned, covering her mouth.

"That was what?" He used his fingers to turn her face. His greatly amused, enchanted eyes searched hers as if the answer to her question meant the world to him.

"That was . . . everything." She felt her cheeks heat. "And I'd like to do it again?" She forced herself to hold his gaze.

His eyes darkened and he kissed her, but only for a moment. "That is a promise." He rested his forehead against hers. "Of more. Ever more."

She nodded, catching her breath after so short a kiss.

"And now I must confess something to you. I admit to not planning for us to kiss just yet." He seemed at once uncomfortable. But then he chuckled, and it set her at ease.

"Is that your confession?" She placed a hand at the side of his face.

"No, not that. But now that I have started, I must tell you all, everything you wish to know."

She paid attention, almost holding her breath for his next words.

The sounds of horses behind them interrupted the moment. "Lord Wilmington!" someone shouted. Someone familiar.

He groaned and she turned slowly. "Is that . . . the Fenningways?"

The three from their household, including their mother and a hoard of servants, approached, their horses trudging through the deep snow, moving rolling folds of powder out to their front.

"Did she just call you Lord Wilmington?" Odette turned to him, half afraid. Truth and shame filled his expression. And then everything showered in on top of her, all the similarities, all the missing invitations, all the holes in both their stories. Everything she should have seen plain as day in front of her face paraded about there, making fun. "Are you?" She sat back, daring him to lie to her.

"It was what I was trying to tell you just now. I am the Marquis of Wilmington."

"And who is Mr. Wardlow?"

"Me as well."

She started shaking her head, but he held up a hand. "Please hear me out."

But the Fenningways were upon them.

"Oh, it is so good to see you, my lord. And I'm so pleased you are not trapped or stuck out here in the middle of our fields." Mrs. Fenningway fanned herself.

Were they on the Fenningway property? They must be. Odette didn't think there could be a worse place to be.

Mr. Wardlow—no, Lord Wilmington—smiled a mostly charming smile. And she realized he could be whomever he needed to be. He could be Mr. Wardlow. He could be the charming lad of the tenants. He could be Lord Wilmington. But who was he really? She moved further from him.

His quick glance in her direction told her he noticed.

Good.

The shock was turning to anger at this point. And suddenly, all she wished to do was be away from him. She turned to the Fenningways. "I'm so glad you've come, actually. We were just talking about a certain dilemma we're having. I could use a way back to my home, while Lord Wilmington must go on in the sleigh."

Both sisters clamored at once with desires to ride in the sleigh.

Odette didn't look again at Lord Wilmington. She didn't want to see him, and she definitely didn't want him to see her. Did he deserve to know she was hurt? Did she want him to know how vulnerable she was around him? No. She did not.

After such a kiss, after feeling like she'd found her future, the betrayal cut deep.

Soon, Lord Wilmington was surrounded by giggling women, and Odette was on top of a horse. She dipped her head to the group. "I thank you. Enjoy the ride. The snow is glorious, isn't it?"

The girls laughed louder, and Odette left the lot of them to themselves. She stuck to the tracks already made by the initial approach of the Fenningways, and the horse was able to manage quite well. But her heart felt torn. Her head ached. Her lips tingled still from his touch, but that tingle felt painful in its reminder. She was done. Done with him and his lies. She sobbed out her thoughts. Did the universe hear thoughts? They were certainly a shout in her mind and could not be ignored.

CHAPTER 19

*H*enry knew he'd lost Odette. But he couldn't face that thought. He had to win her back. He had to do something.

His servants had delivered flowers three times that day— Christmas Day—and he could feel no cheer. He could not revel in the Yule log nor in the food the servants had created just for him. He did take a moment to read the Bible, as his father had done every Christmas. But all thoughts were focused on his terrible treatment of the best lady he'd ever known. He knew her grandmother had encouraged him to continue in his deception, but that was no excuse. And he'd begun it, hadn't he? Why on earth—why had he introduced himself as Mr. Wardlow? Why?

He could only remember that at that moment, he was afraid —afraid of his title, afraid of his responsibility. He'd just returned from off his ship, and he didn't want to be the marquis yet. But that was no excuse. Not now, anyway, after he'd let the lie perpetuate for so long when feelings had run so deep.

He paced his front room.

This was no good.

At least he could smile about how he was assisting Odette

with the Boxing Day celebrations. Perhaps he should stay far away, just send the servants, so as not to ruin her event.

He ran a hand through his hair. What a mess he was in.

A servant approached. "An express for you. The rider awaits a response."

"Thank you." He ripped open and read a hastily written note from his manager in London. The captain was still not coming back, and some of the crew was thinking of leaving with him. The supercargo was abrasive, apparently, and they were tired of dealing with him. Things were falling apart all around him.

"Tell the rider to come in, have a meal, some cider, and relax for a bit while I ponder my next steps."

"Yes, my lord." The servant bowed and left the room.

Again, Henry knew he should leave. Last year, he would have departed without thought. His business required him to. This messy fire needed to be put out, and quickly. But he knew if he left that day, without talking to Odette, he might lose her forever.

And he couldn't bear that thought.

There was a chance, with time, she would grow to forgive him, to trust him again. He must know if she thought such a thing was possible.

Another servant approached. "This has just come from the Goodson home."

He lifted it, feeling the weight of possibility as he tore it open.

Mrs. Goodson had written, *Please come at your earliest convenience.*

He pocketed the note and walked out the front door. It was a good walk to their house. Even with the estates abutting, there was some significant space between their homes, but he'd walked it many times. And he needed the delay in arrival to clear his head. He felt he was perhaps being offered an olive leaf, some sort of peaceful branch. He must snatch it up as thoroughly as he was able. He must prove himself, say . . . what could he say? Whatever was necessary to help Odette see his heart. Hopefully, Mrs. Goodson would support him. He suspected she would.

His heart hammered the whole of his walk.

The snow was high. His decision to cut through their seldom-used property was a poor one. And instead of it being a shortcut, the walk was considerably longer. The tops of his boots were snow filled and his hands red with cold by the time he arrived at their front door.

The butler's eyes widened and the housekeeper exclaimed, "Goodness, boy, come in and warm yourself." She reddened. "Forgive me. I think I will always see you as the marquis's son."

"Yes, I'm afraid that is how I see myself."

A servant approached, and soon his boots were removed from his feet, a blanket draped over his shoulders, and a warm cup placed in his hands while sitting in front of their ample and toasty fire.

Then Odette entered the room.

He jerked to his feet, the blanket dropping on the floor. "Odette, I . . ."

Grandmother followed closely behind.

He bowed smartly. "Miss Goodson, Mrs. Goodson."

They both curtseyed.

"Lord Wilmington. It is always an honor to have you in our home." Mrs. Goodson's formality sharpened the worry he held, but comforted at the same time.

"I'm grateful for your note inviting me."

Odette's gaze darted to her grandmother and back to him so quickly, he almost missed it, but that glance told him she didn't know he was coming.

Sharp disappointment hurt him further.

Mrs. Goodson lowered herself into a chair, slowly. He could tell her health was still not the best. He waited, and when Odette also sat, he joined them, a bit closer to them than the fire would have been.

"Are you recovered?" Mrs. Goodson looked kindly at him. So he could take comfort in that. Would she assist him in his apologies?

"I am, thank you. Your servants have been most attentive."

"Did you walk?" Odette's eyes traveled over him in what looked to be a quick assessment.

"I did, yes. When I received notice that my presence was requested, I left at once."

"Without coat or proper boots?" Odette's eyebrows rose. But she did not as yet look at all sympathetic.

"Apparently so." He cleared his throat. "I appreciate this audience with the both of you. For in the very act of disclosing my deception, I was discovered. And I wish to make clear that it was my every intent to speak the truth. That I do not normally make a practice of lying, to anyone. And that least of all would I want to be dishonest with the woman I love." He looked into Odette's face, but her eyes were turned down. Mrs. Goodson's eyes were full of sympathy, but she offered no explanations to help defend his position.

"I did not wish to disclose my identity immediately upon arriving, you see. I felt completely at odds with myself. I was overcome with the worst kind of guilt at having missed my mother's last years of life, her funeral. I was overcome with the burdens of my title. I'd tried to avoid them, knew the steward had things well in hand all these years. But now, everything I dreaded was coming to pass. And to have to say the words 'I am the Marquis of Wilmington'—it was too much in those early days." He sighed. He knew it was difficult to understand. He could not even fully understand himself. But there it was.

"And when you then so immediately and forcefully denounced my worst actions, took judgement on the things I myself hated most about my behavior, how could I admit that I, Mr. Wardlow, was in fact the dreaded and loathed marquis?"

Odette lifted her lashes. "Do you not see how I feel worse for hearing those words? All that I said, the worst kinds of reactions —you allowed me to continue on in the face of the man who would most be hurt by them. I feel foolish. I feel as though I've been made fun of. And I feel betrayed. How can I know such a man? Who are you? For you can easily make light and fun with the Fenningways. You are a gentleman to all. You are the beloved lad to my grandmother. The tenants see you as one of their own. To me, you have always been Mr. Wardlow. But who is that? Who?" Her face was flushed and her eyes shining. She turned away. Mrs. Goodson rested a hand over top hers.

"I have always been true to you. Besides the detail of my name, I have been the most me with you."

She pressed her lips together.

He knew he had work to do to prove himself. "Perhaps we might begin again?" He held out his hand.

She studied him and it. "What are you proposing?"

At the word propose, his heart hammered. He would like to be proposing. He knew he wanted this lovely, noble woman in his life. But now was not the time to make mention. "Perhaps a turn about the grand hall?"

Her mouth twitched and then she allowed a slow smile to fill her face. "Very well." She placed her hand in his. They stood. "I shall return, Grandmother."

"Oh, don't mind me. I suppose I shall entertain myself." She lifted a book. "With this light, I can still see just fine."

"Perhaps we can return and read to you?" Henry smiled at her. His heart warmed toward the dear woman. And he hoped she would return to better health.

"I'd like that, thank you."

Henry tucked Odette's hand into the crook of his arm as they left the room. "Thank you."

"For our walk?"

"Yes, and for giving me a chance."

She didn't answer for a moment, but then she puffed out a bit of air. "You are too charming."

He tried not to laugh victoriously at her frustration but failed.

"You think that is a point in your favor, but it is really a statement of distrust. You could charm anyone. You have worked your magic on me. And now I don't know who I'm talking to."

"I will prove it to you. I have been only myself. With everyone. Have you considered that the same man who is appreciated by the Fenningways and is friends with the tenants is also the man who has neglected his duty all these years?"

She looked away for a long moment. "Yes, I suppose that could be."

"It is the truth. I am me, Henry." He dipped his head to try and catch her eye as they walked side by side. "Henry. I have always been Henry with you."

She didn't say anything, but stepped a bit closer. He didn't know if that was on purpose, but he was happy with any small victories.

They entered the great hall. Wood carvings lined the ceiling, and painted murals of hunting scenes filled the room.

"This is in truth a great hall."

Her mouth twitched.

"Ah, see, that was humorous."

Her smile grew. "You are funny, yes."

They walked to the center of the room and then he bowed. "May I have this dance?"

"What?" She eyed him with a growing amusement.

"Yes, right now, with no music. I would like to dance with you." He bowed, and then held out his hand.

"Oh, very well." Odette laughed and placed her hand in his palm. "But this does not change anything."

"Oh, I hope not."

They turned, bowed and curtseyed, and then turned away, making the steps to a common minuet.

"You hope not?"

"Certainly, where would be the fun in missing out on this grand opportunity to win your hand, to finally be the Marquis of Wilmington with you?"

"I . . . I don't know."

"You see? I have only been permitted to impress you with half my abilities. Now, I might at last convince you of my undying devotion with the full resources behind me."

They turned to each other and circled.

"Does that not sound pleasant?" he asked.

"It . . . might."

"Will I see you at the Boxing Day celebrations?"

"Yes, of course, and might I take this moment to thank you? The marquis . . . your contributions to the day have not gone unnoticed."

"Ah, you see? Already, I might have the honor of proving my worth to you."

They continued in their steps, Henry teasing, luring her out of her distrust, Odette succumbing only slightly. But progress was progress, and his hope grew.

CHAPTER 20

*O*dette didn't know what to think. She knew what she felt: hurt. However, trust for Henry came naturally. Curse her feelings. She loved him. But had she fallen in love with someone who didn't exist? How could she know for sure?

She needed time. But even then . . .

Today was Boxing Day. And today she would focus on the tenants, the servants, and the community. It looked as though Grandmother might even be able to attend some of the festivities. Their Christmas Eve had been quiet, and that was nice. But Boxing Day would be full of people, friends, and others, and Odette needed that too.

She'd spent the day in preparations with the shop owners, who were as excited as she. The silk throwers would be there doing demonstrations, and they'd even found a theater troupe that was near to put on some performances. It promised to be a grand day, indeed. And with the marquis—Henry's—aid, every person would have a gift. Many were bringing gifts as well to trade, but in the case of someone not able to provide something, there were ample extras.

Odette was just about ready to depart. She found her grandmother, who had decided she would come on her own if she could manage. "Thank you, Grandmother. For allowing me to follow my heart in this."

"Your heart is in a good place." She reached up and placed a hand on the side of Odette's face. "I love you, child. I have raised you as my own."

"I love you, too, Grandmother." She gathered her grandmother's hands in her own and held them. "Would you believe Henry?"

"Why don't you have a seat for a moment?" She patted the chair at her side.

"What is it?"

"I just want to tell you something. When Lord Wilmington came to our home, you recall that I played along with his ruse?"

She frowned. "I recall now. Why did you do such a thing?"

"He even returned to admit all, but I convinced him to wait."

"You did?" She studied her grandmother's kind face. "Why?"

"I knew you weren't ready. You were going to hate him all the more because you were wrong. And you still thought the worst of that poor man."

"Poor man, indeed."

"He is. He's orphaned, same as you, but he doesn't have a grandmother to care for him. He doesn't have anyone but those he pays and the kind folks in this town. And he has all the responsibility in the world heaped on his shoulders. Do you know how old he was when people started looking to him as the marquis?"

Odette shook her head, thinking through the math.

"Twelve."

She nodded. "That's young."

"It is. And then he was shipped off to school. He has had no time to acclimate to the title here at home. It means something to be the Marquis of Wilmington, and I think sometimes that knowledge is too much."

"And so you think he was right to conceal his identity?"

"No. I don't blame him, that first encounter, but I think he should have been brave and confessed the minute you started complaining about him."

Odette blushed. "I was ridiculous."

"And you weren't of a mind to hear anything contrary to what you were certain you knew."

"So you told Henry to wait, to first show me some positive qualities in the marquis?" She remembered her opinion of the man had changed.

"More than that. He started having dinner parties, planned a ball even. That man has been doing everything for you since the day he met you."

"Oh." She hadn't guessed as much. "And my opinion of the marquis has changed. You know it has."

"Yes, but he was not able to wait a moment longer. He planned your sleigh ride to tell all. Would you have felt differently about the news had he told you before you discovered it?"

She nodded slowly. "I might have, yes. But I cannot imagine I would have been pleased either way."

"No, I imagine not. But you can at least see he deserves a bit of our mercy?"

"I suppose. Do you trust him?"

"I think so? I haven't known him since he was young, but that same goodness that shone in his face as a young lad is still there now. I think he is one of the best men you will ever meet, mistake or no."

"And the Season?"

"Well now, that all depends. If you don't agree to court that man here, we will have to follow him to London, make no mistake."

"Oh, you are too horrid." She laughed and then kissed her grandmother's cheek. "I must go. But I'll consider all you've said. I do love him, you know. Whether that's a curse or not, I cannot say."

"I think you'll know soon enough."

"Certainly bears considering, doesn't it?"

"Enjoy yourself, dearie. I do believe you've created a new town tradition."

Odette smiled all the way to her carriage. A new town tradition. Of families coming together. Of gatherings during Christmastime. Perhaps she'd made a difference in Cheshire. She pulled up to the town, and already so many had gathered that there wasn't much room to walk through the main area to the fountain. But everywhere she turned were people to greet and enjoy. Her servants were here, not in livery. The scullery maid walked around on the arm of one of the footmen. Odette smiled. Their butler and housekeeper stood side by side.

Everything was as it should be. Odette's smile started to ache on her face, but she grinned ever wider. Then the shop owners arrived, and to Odette's pleased surprise, they brought their wares out onto the street. People walked from one to another, talking and sharing and wishing each other well.

Mr. Hughes stood up on the fountain. "And now, the Marquis of Wilmington wants to say a word."

Odette gasped. Her heart sped up, and even though she tried not to, she loved that man. Just loved him. He stood tall, a strong, confident leader in their community. He waved at everyone in such a humble manner that she also found him endearing. How could a man be both confident and humble? She was seeing it right now, and it was working. Every person around her turned their shining, appreciative eyes to him. She imagined she looked the same. They stopped talking.

"I wanted to wish everyone a Merry Christmas."

Great cheers went up from the crowd.

"And I think some thanks are in order."

They cheered again.

"To the Hughes family, thank you for organizing all the shop owners."

He went on and on, knowing and understanding all the major players to this activity. He listed them all. And Odette was quite amazed at his awareness.

"And we would not be complete until we thank the one who made this whole evening possible. To the woman who wants more than anything to have friends who are family, to have a community of people who love and share and celebrate together. To our own Miss Odette Goodson."

Everyone turned to her. Even people she didn't know knew her, and they clapped and cheered. Then someone nudged her forward.

And Henry waved her over.

She swallowed twice and then made her way to the front through the crowd. With a gentle wipe of a few tears, she stood in front of them all, next to Henry. "What have you done?"

"I thought you would like to speak to them."

"You were right." She sniffed. "But I didn't know it until now."

His eyes beamed with pleasure. "Happy to hear it." He gestured to the crowd. "What do you want to say to all these good people?"

"I know just the thing." She faced them. "Thank you for this. My parents passed away years ago, and I came to live with the Goodsons, my grandparents. And now it's just my grandmother and me. Most of the time, we are perfectly content. But around Christmas, I, we both, miss being around a group of family. You know, I had a dream once, that everyone I knew and loved was all in one place celebrating. That we had the best party Cheshire has ever been known to have."

They clapped and cheered.

"And as I look out at all of you, I know that my dreams have come true. Thank you for making it happen. Thank you one and all."

They cheered again. And then out of nowhere, music.

"What?"

The crowd parted, and a small group of musicians played.

"Surprise." Henry grinned and held out his hand. "Might I have this dance?"

People all around her were pairing off, and a line had formed in two different places to accommodate more. It was the perfect idea for their gathering, and she was thrilled he'd made it happen.

She rested her hand in his. "With pleasure." They stepped together and joined the end of the line.

But as soon as they stepped up, the rest of the line then turned to them to lead, so they went through the first steps of the dance. While the others down the line repeated, Henry stepped closer to her at his side. "I would be happy doing exactly this with you for the rest of my days."

She sucked in a breath. Dare she look at him?

"Odette." His deep voice rolled through her heart, shaking things up as it went.

When she dared a glance at his face, his eyes were full of sincerity, and his lips . . .

She looked away. His lips reminded her of all the ways she knew that mouth. And that was something she didn't want to be thinking of in this moment, or ever again.

Ever again? Was she to never again kiss Lord Wilmington? Saying his real name was no real hardship. And she'd already come to almost respect the marquis. She'd certainly repented of having thought so ill of him. So was it so terribly bad that he'd pretended to be a commoner? Certainly, far worse if he'd pretended nobility.

She didn't know. She wished he hadn't pretended anything.

They danced four dances, and she thought that these were

probably going to be her most enjoyed dances of all. She didn't even care that she danced only with him. Very few of the gentlemen families had attended, and the shop owners, tenants, and servants danced with whom they liked. She'd heard that in London, you were permitted to dance with one person only two times. They'd never stuck so rigidly to that rule in Cheshire. The ladies at Odette's finishing school would not agree with such a disregard for societal norms.

But Odette thought it grand. She forgot for a time that she was hurt by Henry. She forgot that she was supposed to distrust him and just enjoyed his company. Something about him was more free. He was more demonstrative of his caring. And he was certainly more attentive to her.

When the music at last stopped and people were lingering quietly or making their way home, she walked with her hand on his arm. "Thank you for the music. It was the best part of the night."

"I don't know. I think the best part of the night gifted me a sack full of items from the bakery."

"Oh, true. That might be the best part of my night if it happened to me as well."

"I am in jest, of course. Would you like to know my true best part of the night?" He stopped and turned to her.

They stood close. His face was lit by the lantern behind them, the light flickering on his features.

"If you'd like to tell me."

"I would." He lifted her hand to his lips. "This, right now, is the best part of my night." His eyes captured hers. She could not look away even if she wanted to. He kissed her hand again. "And the moment right before now, and the moment before that."

"I'm sensing a pattern here." She tried to make light, the barest chuckle leaving her throat. Her mouth was dry, her eyes watching his lips as they kissed her hand again.

"Every moment with you is my best part, Odette."

She lifted her lashes to see him again. They stood closer. She was practically in his arms. And she never wanted to leave.

"I . . ." He closed his eyes. "If this is too soon, forgive me, but I cannot stay my mouth. Please, Odette. I don't deserve you, but I will work every day for the rest of my life to do so. I love you. Please, put me out of my misery and be my wife?" He lowered to one knee, watching her face as though she held his life in her hands.

Her heartbeat pounded through her. The world wobbled for a moment, and she worried that for the first time in her life, she would faint. But then it cleared, and she knew. "You wish to go to London."

He opened his mouth and then closed it, and then his shoulders lowered. "I do. In fact, I'm very needed there right now, but I couldn't leave without speaking with you first."

She looked around at who might be watching. They were alone. "Please stand."

He did so, and the hurt in his eyes caused an ache deep inside. "This doesn't bode well."

"I love you too."

"That's better?" The hope in his face had dimmed.

"I don't want to go to London."

"You don't have to go now. Or do you mean ever?"

"Ever. I wish to stay here in Cheshire. I wish to live with these people. They are my family. London has nothing for me."

"Would you like to consider my offer, take some time—"

She shook her head. "I'm sorry, but no. I'm afraid I cannot marry you." She choked on the last word, as though its presence in her mouth, its spoken existence, were causing her pain. "I belong here, and you obviously . . . don't." She turned from him. Where was her carriage?

Down the street, her loyal servant, her footman, stood waiting.

She raised her hand, and he stepped up on the carriage, which moved in her direction.

When she turned back to Henry, he was sad indeed. His face was drawn, tired, hopeless. Gone was the light of heart, the twinkle, and she thought that worst of all. "I'm sorry."

He nodded.

When her carriage pulled up beside them, he helped her up and bowed his farewells, but his face was a mask, and his eyes looked elsewhere.

As they pulled away, her soft whisper would never reach him. "Goodbye."

CHAPTER 21

*H*enry probably shouldn't have been surprised, but he was. He shouldn't have been offended, but he was. And now he was hurriedly packing everything he owned in several trunks to head to London. He was long overdue.

Twelfth Night could be celebrated there as well as here. And he'd absolutely done his duty by this town. No one could fault him or call him the Missing Marquis any longer. He'd bought the whole town Christmas presents.

His jaw was sore from all the clenching of his teeth, but he was doing it again. Odette had turned him down. Outright. With no thought. Even though he was the blooming marquis. In the one moment it should have assisted his case, his title hadn't seemed to matter one whit to her. He remembered the words of his father, as he was leaving for Eton. *"Your coming title will ease your way in many instances. Friends will come easier. Marriage might. But in the case of marrying, be sure to find a woman who is interested in the man behind the title."* He'd winked and then added, *"And be interesting."* Of course, in the case of Odette, she'd been more disturbed by his title than anything.

He marched to the front door, following a long procession of trunks. His servants had gathered as requested. He cleared his throat. "Many of you have been with me since I was a young lad. We've had a good time of it this holiday, but now I go again. To London. I cannot be certain when I will return, but I'd like to wish you well for Twelfth Night. And thank you"—he cleared his throat—"for once again maintaining the Wilmington estate whilst all Wardlows are not present."

The gazes that returned his belonged to kind, loyal, good people. He clipped his heels and walked out the door. They would be fine. They always had been. The ball would be canceled. He'd tasked Mrs. Taylor with sending his regrets to all who had been invited. The servants were gifted the food and wine that had already been purchased for the event. They might be more pleased than anything that he was gone.

As he drove away, deliberately not looking out the window, he had to ask himself: Would he be fine?

And he didn't know the answer.

Certainly, he would function. He would aid in his business. He would grow his estate. He might pay a visit to Whites, his father's gentleman club. But those were necessities. Would he be well? He lifted the fabric that covered his window and saw, as they were turning away, a final glimpse of the tall pines that filled the Goodson land. To him, they would always be Odette's pines, as she loved them so. He knew that without her in his life, he would not be fine.

He snapped the covering back down. But she'd refused him. There was no sense pining after a woman who would not have him.

ODETTE WATCHED out the window as Henry's carriage rolled past her house. He didn't even look, not one last time, nothing. But she watched until he turned the corner and was gone from sight, and then sat in a deflated heap. Had she turned down the man she loves?

The day passed as if in a dream. She sat with her grandmother in the morning room while they read books. She finished a needlepoint she'd worked on these past two years. She ordered dinners for the week and planned a few Twelfth Night festivities. But she felt nothing. It was as if her life that she had lived happily and satisfactorily until now had lost all flavor. The colors were dull and the smells bland.

Five times, she wondered if Henry would stop by, and she had to remind herself that he was gone. Even a walk sounded like a less than enjoyable pursuit. But she went anyway.

All bundled up yet again so that the cold could not penetrate, she stepped out into the snow. It had crusted over the top, and so for the most part, she was able to walk around on top of its depths. She found herself making her way to the Wilmington estate. It was a well-traveled path for her—she told herself that was why she went. But she knew she hoped to feel closer to her beloved Henry. How did one continue on a path without the one they loved? What did one do when the one they loved wanted a different life than she wanted? Oh goodness. London was never in her plans. Living with him far from Cheshire sounded . . . scary.

She puffed out a breath. She was afraid.

The longer she walked along, the warmer she became. She started to peel off items of clothing. She wanted the cold to penetrate. She wanted to feel something, anything other than this menial existence of indifference to all things that used to bring her happiness. Once her earmuffs were off, she felt the bite of the icy air, and with exhilarated satisfaction, smiled into the wind that had picked up. "I will conquer this," she told the pines.

If only she could be like the pines, towering, strong in the face of every kind of resistance. Nothing could stop them in their upward growth. What had they seen? Generations of Goodsons and Wardlows living side by side. Had their ancestors ever wondered if a Goodson and a Wardlow would unite?

She kept walking. A bridge between their properties waited ahead. It was the path she'd taken the first time she'd met her Mr. Wardlow. She smiled, almost tenderly. Things were much simpler when she thought herself enamored with a gentleman farmer. That life would have been much simpler. Not much would have changed from the life she now lived with her grandmother. Except for children, and family.

Her heart ached.

She wished for family. People all around her, filled with love. Children. She hugged herself. Would it be so difficult to imagine a family in London? Would they not ever come to Cheshire? Of course they would.

Her heart pounded within her. Was she still considering his offer?

He'd left without many kind expressions. Perhaps the offer was not still available to her. Refusing someone's hand in marriage seemed permanent.

She walked out across the small bridge that crossed over into his estate. Her boots echoed with the sound of striking wood instead of the soft snow. She stopped at the center and peered down into the water. The banks were full of crusty ice, bits of the calm waters that had frozen, but the center rushed stubbornly on in the face of the ice, in defiance to the chill that would stop its course. She reached down to pick up a stick at her feet and dropped it into the water. It rushed past in the greatest hurry. She knew not where it would end up. The stick was off on a grand adventure even it could not predict.

Had she not at one point wished for adventure? She leaned back against the bridge railing, resting her elbows and looking up to the tops of the pines all around her. Back when she was young, while her parents were still alive, she'd dreamed of a grand boat journey. Her father had even promised her one once she was older. *"You shall travel. I'll take you myself to the grand salons in Paris."*

But she'd longed for more, the great open sea, the feeling of not knowing where she would end up. Her parents had found a painting of a grand ship and placed it in her room. She'd dreamed of the water in those days. Yearned for adventure.

And then she'd lost her parents, been sent to Cheshire and then off to finishing school. And that was all the adventure she needed. Instead, she'd longed for familiarity.

But now? How long would Grandmother last to remain her companion? And when she left? Where was Odette's familiarity? She realized now she'd counted on Cheshire. They would become her family, her friends. She closed her eyes. Henry.

His face filled her memory, his laughing eyes, his tender smile, his tall, strong presence at her side. His kisses . . .

She ran fingers along her lips. His kisses.

Love for Henry burned within her. She cried out, and rested her head on her hands, watching tears fall into the river below. They seemed to be unnoticed by the great rush around them, carried along, alone.

The walk back to her home was long and sad and slow. Her feet trudged through sometimes large banks. The sun had come out and softened the snow enough to prevent her walking along the top in areas.

By the time she arrived at the back servants' entrance, she was wet through.

"Goodness, child." The cook scurried about until she had a tray with hot tea and warm soup. "Please warm yourself here."

Odette nodded. "Thank you." The liquids did much to stop the quivering from cold. Once she'd eaten enough that she thought she could change out of her wet things, she made her way to her rooms.

As soon as she stepped in the door, her maid began removing

her outer things. The fire had been built up and the room was at once cozy. Without even giving it a second thought, she climbed into bed, her feet surrounded by warming pans, and piled on the blankets. She was soon drifting off to sleep.

When she awoke, the sun still streamed through her windows, but she could tell it was later in the afternoon. For a moment, she fought off reality, stubbornly determined to remain in her half-awake dream of happiness. But as the realities from yesterday seeped into her awareness, she pulled the covers up tighter around her.

"You can't hide, you know."

She gasped and lifted her head. "Grandmother?"

"Hello, my dear. Are you well?" She placed a hand on Odette's forehead. "Not feverish." She spoke to someone in the doorway.

Odette peered over to see the doctor nod and then leave.

"You called Mr. Green?"

"Certainly. Arriving in the bitter cold, missing half your outer clothing and wet through." She clucked. But Odette could see relief had lightened the dear woman's face.

"I'm sorry to cause alarm."

"Don't you worry one bit. We are just pleased your constitution has weathered it just fine."

"I wish to stay here forever."

"In bed?"

She nodded, and then squinted her eyes against a tear that threatened. It fell anyway, and her grandmother wiped it with her softest of all hands.

"How are your hands so soft?"

"Rosewater, they say." She laughed. "But I'm glad you think so."

"I'm glad we have each other."

"So am I. You have been a light in my later years that I would have sorely missed."

"I was thinking, perhaps we could go to London after all?"

Grandmother's eyes twinkled. "Were you?"

"Yes, you know, just to see what a Season is like." The grin she tried to hide broke free. And then she pulled the covers over her head. "But I'm so afraid. Why can we not just stay here?"

"You are not afraid. Not really. I know life has been hard. I know you crave the familiar. I know you pine for your parents. Of course you do. But there's a part of you still that will only be happy if you are exploring." She pulled back the covers to free Odette's face and ran a finger along her hairline, clearing all errant strands. "Perhaps you're nervous. But can you find that bold and brazen Odette who stubbornly climbed every tree in the place so she could see what more there was to the world besides these old trees and a couple almost as old?" Grandmother laughed tenderly.

Memories flooded back. Of an Odette who felt cramped, trapped by the giants around them, an Odette who longed to see the world. A scared Odette who quaked in their presence when she felt completely alone. She could see how her desires to be sheltered had come upon her.

"Is that person still here somewhere?" She placed a hand at her heart, as if it could discover the mysteries of her soul by being there.

"Of course she is." Grandmother pulled back the covers. "Look what I've found."

Odette followed her gaze and then shot up in bed. The old painting, of the ship, was now hanging on her bedroom wall. "Where did you find this?"

The ship was tall and brilliant, the waves white tipped and all around that ship. And on the bow stood a girl with her hands in the air, the wind whipping her hair.

Odette walked to the painting and put her finger up on that girl's head just as she used to. "Is this who I really am?"

Grandmother put her arm around Odette, pulling her close to

171

her side as they both studied the work. "She's in there, but so is the woman who cared for the town, the girl who minds her grandmother. So many dear qualities reside all together in the one heart that beats in your chest."

Odette knew she was right. "I could be anything, couldn't I?"

"You could."

They stood side by side. Odette didn't know how long. Her mind was racing through all the possibilities. A happy, secure life here at home, the life she thought Mr. Wardlow offered. A happy, adventurous life with Lord Wilmington, one she couldn't even predict or envision in her mind, except for him. His face returned to her mind, strong, handsome.

She could run to him. She could go to London. Grandmother had a situation for them. The thought filled her with a new and buoyant exhilaration, something she hadn't felt in a long time. But Grandmother was not fully well. She needed rest.

"Well." She took a deep breath. "We have Twelfth Night celebrations to consider at any rate, don't we?" She turned and kissed her grandmother on the cheek.

"And then we can talk about this nonsense of traveling and such."

The small laugh that shook her grandmother made Odette smile. "I bet you think you had something to do with this match, don't you?"

Her smile turned secretive. "I just might have."

DEAR EUOTA

December 25, 1815

My dearest Euota,

I think I've seen a softening in Odette. She was hurt, as she had every right to be, but in this match, she's found herself again. And I rejoice in that potential. To find a match that also brings out your true self is a treasure indeed.

Now, if we can only convince Lord Wilmington to propose yet again. I think he will. He doesn't seem the sort to hold a grudge or cling too tightly to his pride, but I cannot predict. Who am I to understand a man's heart? He was likely hurt by her refusal.

I am growing stronger. The doctor has just proclaimed I am free to travel after Twelfth Night. So it is off to London we go. I cannot wait to fill your letters with the details of the Season, as all will remind me of you and the others. A Merry Christmas to you, my friend.

Yours,
Amelie

CHAPTER 22

*H*enry walked through the ship, the captain at his side. He'd convinced the man to return, and together they'd found a new supercargo. Completing an inspection, he felt proud of all he'd accomplished. The great masts rose up to the night sky. The water lapped against the side of the boat. The wood beneath his feet felt smooth with years of weather. And of all this, he was owner.

"I'm a bit sheepish making you come all the way here before Twelfth Night and all." The captain turned to him. "But I appreciate you hearing me out. And I think everyone will be happier with the new man we picked."

"You're a valuable part of the team. I trust you. We have a busy year, and I'll be needing help finding more captains even, come the end of it."

"Yes, my lord. I'll be on the lookout for them as well."

They made their way to the exit ramp. Henry would be sleeping on board, and the captain was going home to his family.

"I'll be seeing you, then?" Henry tipped his hat.

"Yes, you will."

Henry stayed up on deck. He moved to the other railing,

away from the lights on the docks, looking for the stars. There was nothing like a sky full of stars out in the middle of the water. Nothing at all, especially on those clear nights with hardly a roll to the ocean. The world was vast and undiscovered. The opportunities were endless. And the wealth almost limitless as well. He rested his forearms on the railing. But what did any of it matter?

She'd refused him.

He should be exalting in every little thing around him, in the very fact that he stood on a boat that was part of a shipping business of his own making. But he could not. Somehow, in the moments they'd had together in Cheshire, Odette had captured his heart in such a way that nothing mattered anymore if she were not in it.

He'd tried to push onward. He'd made the rounds at Whites and to the few people he knew in Town. He'd been invited places. But what he really wanted was waiting for him in Cheshire.

And he couldn't have that life.

Or could he? A new vision of what his life could be started to map itself in his mind. Perhaps it wasn't what he'd always dreamed, journeys on his boat to exotic places, but it was a good, sweet life. A quiet life.

He smiled, a glimmer of hope flickering like a candle caught in a draft.

ODETTE PACED the floor in her room. Today was Twelfth Night. Today, she would celebrate alone with her grandmother. They had planned to eat their favorite foods, read their favorite books, and play their favorite Twelfth Night games even if it was just for the two of them. She had asked Cook to hide a bean in the cake. They would bring out the burning brandy. And Odette

A SLEIGH RIDE KISS

would sing and play the pianoforte. It would be a festive night indeed, if a little lonely.

She tried to push the thoughts aside, but pangs for her parents, her grandfather, and any family at all filled her as they had threatened to the entire season. And most of all, a great, vast loneliness for Henry dominated all other thought.

Oh, how she craved his company.

She made her way to her grandmother's room. "I've decided we should leave tomorrow." She spoke the words as she entered the bedroom, but her grandmother was asleep with the candles still lit, a book opened across her chest.

She appeared older while resting there than she did when vibrancy lit her face. But peace hovered about her and smoothed her lines. She was a dear, a giant of a woman at the same time that she was fragile. Grandmother had kept up a festive spirit all day, Odette was certain, to appease her. And now the woman was exhausted.

Odette sighed. Well, she was perfectly happy to share their meal with the servants, something her grandmother was much too proper and formal to do often.

She marked her grandmother's spot, closed the book, and blew out the candles. They could do their other activities tomorrow.

As she stepped down the stairs, the quiet echoed. And she knew she would not be traveling to London tomorrow. How could she? Grandmother needed to recover still. She tried to make do with what she had, like she'd always done. She tried to find the good, list out the happy pieces of her moment, but suddenly, the task was too much. She moved more and more slowly, until she gripped the railing in her pain and doubled over her stomach. The sobs came out as silently as she could manage, but they wracked her body. Her head pounded; tears poured down her face. Nothing. There was nothing good about today. Twelfth Night, and she was utterly alone. She'd turned down the one man she'd ever loved. She might lose him altogether. She could not go to him in the near future, nor write to him, and she would be having a meal fit for ten with the servants. As she sucked in her breath between sobs, the front door opened.

Boots entered the hall. She wished to retreat, but there was nothing for it—whomever had come to wish them well would see her in much need of well wishing.

She lifted her wet lashes.

Henry stepped forward, his face pained, his hand outstretched. Their butler slipped away. Henry took one step forward. "Odette."

She choked out some sort of greeting and ran the rest of the way down the stairs to him. "Henry." She fell into his arms, the sobs continuing. She clung to him, burying her face in his shoulder until a semblance of peace filled her.

He handed her a handkerchief, which she used, then lifted her face to him. "You've come."

His own eyes were wet. Had he cried for her? She lifted a finger to brush away the moisture.

"I'm here." He lifted her up into his arms. "Where shall I take you?" His eyes sparkled with the same familiar light he carried.

"How about by the fire?"

"Very good." He nodded and walked them toward the double doors.

A footman opened them.

"Thank you, Thomas." Odette smiled.

He winked at her and then faced forward.

"Cheeky footman." Henry grinned.

"Not at all. He's a dear."

Henry placed her on a settee for two and then sat as close as he could beside her. "Now, tell me the cause of so much sadness."

She leaned into him. "You've solved it already. I'm quite cured."

"Are you?" His eyes, as perceptive as ever, looked deep inside.

"I don't know. I was just so very lonely. Grandmother fell asleep before our dinner even, before any of our planned activities, and I was on my own."

"I'm sorry I left."

"I'm sorry I turned you down."

"You are?"

She nodded. "So very sorry. When what I want most in this world is to have a family, I sent away the only other person who could make it so."

"The only other?"

"Certainly. For I love you. I would not want to marry anyone else but you. And I do hope I've not lost my chance." She watched him closely. His face seemed hesitant, almost fearful, but there was something there, a light, that gave her hope.

He immediately dropped to his knees. "Then I ask again, my dearest, loveliest, most wonderful Odette, please do me the honor of being my wife?"

She burst into tears again, this time in celebration for so many of the torn, ripped parts inside stitching themselves together in that moment. "Yes. Henry, it doesn't matter to me where we live, as long as I'm with you. I will marry you. Of course. Tomorrow, if we can."

"Really? You've decided to come to London?"

"I'll come aboard your ship. Wherever you go, I go."

"Might we also live here?"

"In Cheshire?"

"Yes, I've worked it out so that the larger portion of the year, we will spend here at home. And then for parts of the busiest times, we could go to London to handle things there. If anything comes up between, I can always make my own trips to take care of things."

She hiccupped. "Oh dear, excuse me. You would do that for me?"

"I would. I discovered on this wretched trip to London that I would do anything for you."

Odette wrapped her arms around his neck, squeezing with all she had. "And I would do the same for you." She pulled away. "Do you know what I remembered?"

"What is that?"

"I used to long to travel by boat."

"Did you?"

"I most certainly did. I have a grand painting to prove it."

"I don't understand."

"Oh, I'll explain it all over dinner. You are staying, aren't you?"

"I most certainly am. I wouldn't miss Twelfth Night with the only family I have."

She laughed. "We are so alike, you know."

"I do believe you are right in that." Henry stood and pulled a wrapped parcel out of his pocket. "Perhaps this gift is at last appropriate."

She gently peeled back the papers wrapping a small package. "A gift." She smiled. When at last a curious box was revealed, she glanced up at him in question.

"Wind it." He indicated a small key.

When the box began to play music to a waltz, she was lost to its wonder.

He held out a hand. "Dance with me?"

Then stepping closer than she ever had, she rested a hand on his shoulder, on his arm and allowed him to circle her around their small parlor. "I hope we spend many evenings doing just this."

He kissed her forehead. "I too have the same wish. And now, there is only one thing remaining."

"And what is that?" She lifter her chin to see into his eyes.

"Something I've been thinking about ever since the first time I kissed you." He wrapped his arms around her, pulling her as close as she could be. She waited, her whole body tingling in expectation. "If our first kiss was so blessedly wonderful, what will our second one be like?" he said.

"I think we better find out."

Before he could say another word, she stepped up on her toes and pressed her mouth to his. In an instant, this holiday turned from one of the loneliest of her life to the most precious. In fact, in that one moment, she at last felt like she belonged to someone —wholly and completely and forever belonged.

And that made for the best Twelfth Night of all.

DEAR EUOTA

January 7, 1815

My dearest Euota,

We've done it. No one will hardly credit our ingenuity, but we've accomplished growing unions of great happiness, have we not? My dearest Odette looks happier than even I during my courtship.

The two will be wed. And I only hope to be present and happy at their wedding. Do not be alarmed at my announcement. I am well, truly. But I have been so tired of late that I prefer my chair, or even sometimes my bed. But nothing could make me happier in this grand life of ours than to see my Odette well and joyful and so grandly taken care of. The Goodson and Wardlow estates will join, though it is left to Odette and outside the marriage settlement. It is hers.

How odd to participate in the legal proceedings regarding a woman's marriage, but I'll tell you what I thought. I am determined in my obstinacy that a woman should participate in all such proceedings. For who better to think of her needs and rights than a fellow woman? But no one shall listen to me past the dictates of my guardianship over Odette. And that is perhaps as it should be.

Are we in the December of our lives? If so, it is the grandest of all seasons, is it not?

My love to you, Euota, until we meet.

Amelie

EPILOGUE

$\mathcal{O}$dette and Henry returned to Cheshire County for the promised ball, though postponed, many were still in town because of the huge amounts of snow that had fallen, preventing travel for all who were not so equipped as to own a sleigh.

Odette entered the ball wearing a stunning red dress, saving the gorgeous blues she had purchased for another day.

As they were announced at what had turned into their own wedding celebration, they laughed opened at a sea of women in blue dresses.

Odette turned to Henry. "They are so very dear though, aren't they?"

"Not as dear as the woman at my side."

"When do we depart?" Odette had found a new courage and now looked forward to their voyage to the East Indies above all else.

"As soon as we get some weather worth traveling in." He chuckled. "I cannot wait to show it all to you."

Grandmother's full smile and joy filled faced beamed at her.

With four dear friends at her side, and a ball to honor her grand daughter, there were only more and more reasons to smile.

Her fingers laced with Henry's and she squeezed his strong hand. They would be very happy indeed.

—

Read the next book in the A Christmas Match series: A Yorkshire Carol.

For more Christmas books by Jen Geigle Johnson:

Snow and Mistletoe

A Christmas Kiss

FOR ALL KINDS of news and access to all of Jen's books' sales, follow her HERE.

FOLLOW JEN

Jen's other published books

The Duke's Second Chance
The Earl's Winning Wager
Her Lady's Whims and Whimsies
Suitors for the Proper Miss
Pining for Lord Lockhart
The Foibles and Follies of Miss Grace

The Nobleman's Daughter
Two lovers in disguise

Scarlet
The Pimpernel retold

A Lady's Maid
Can she love again?

His Lady in Hiding
Hiding out as his maid.

Spun of Gold
Rumpelstilskin Retold

Dating the Duke
Time Travel: Regency man in NYC

Charmed by His Lordship
The antics of a fake friendship

Tabitha's Folly
Four over-protective brothers

To read Damen's Secret
The Villain's Romance

Follow her Newsletter